HARLOW STONE

THE UGLY ROSES TRILOGY
BLINDED BY FATE – BOOK THREE

Reviews

I never read a male character with so much raw emotion. Ryder Callaghan has become one of my favorite book boyfriends'. —**JB'S Book Obsession**

I know that at some point in your lives you have ridden a roller coaster, right? Filled with sharp turns, thrilling dips, and breath-taking earth-shattering finales. Well that is what you get when you read this breath-taking series. Harlow's characters grab you and make you their own.
— **The Book Fairy Reviews**

A beautiful finale to an exceptional and incomparable series that it is going to be hard to find anything quite as unique. This is a series I will want to read again and again...bravo Harlow! —**Goodreads Reviewer**

Book two is ...I was speechless. Blown away. It's well written, developing the characters and plot line so that their story was a living entity in my consciousness. Unable to function until I had consumed every word—
Obsessed By Books

Copyright

Blinded By Fate

The Ugly Roses Trilogy III

Written by Harlow Stone

All rights reserved.

ISBN: 978-0-9940376-5-7

Edited by Gregory Murphy

Cover design by Harlow Stone

THE UGLY ROSES

A note from the author,

Not for one second did I believe one book would turn into three. I kept on writing, you kept on reading, and here we are.
The Ugly Roses Trilogy complete.
Readers, you motivate me.
I love each and every one of you.
Thank you for sticking with me.

Much love,

Harlow

xx

Prologue

Two days ago

The prison guard reaches out and grabs me by the front of my shirt, causing it to rip as he hauls me off the bed. I try to cooperate, not wanting to anger him anymore but he slaps my face—probably because I'm not fast enough.

I'm shoved backward into the cold concrete wall. The force causes the air to whoosh out of my lungs and my trembling legs to weaken. Grabbing a fist full of my hair, he holds me upright.

"Stay still."

I don't know why he asks, it's not like I can move. I don't understand until the flash of the camera blinds me once again. I blink, repeatedly, trying to regain my sense of sight.

"You must be popular, princess, or worth something. Because our little photoshoot is over."

He releases my hair, and I let out the breath I was holding, hoping to hell I can now go above ground, and back to my cell. I will my legs to take me there, one foot in front of the other, but his hand moves to my shoulder while his mouth moves to my ear. The sick hushed voice raises the hairs on my neck.

"That doesn't mean I'm done with you."

He moves away from my ear, remaining close enough that I can feel his breath on my cheeks. Regardless of the lack of light, I don't miss the evil smirk on his face. The calloused thumb on his left hand moves from my neck, into the hollow of my collarbone. He applies enough force in the pressure point, using his hand to push down, leaving me no choice but to drop to my knees.

"Now be a good inmate, number 76413."

I'm shocked for a moment before I attempt to pull back, refusing to be belittled or treated like a subject. Still, he continues to push in the tender nerves behind my collarbone, rendering me motionless with his left hand, while his right moves to his belt. He quickly undoes the buckle with practiced speed, while keeping me helpless on my knees.

How did I get here?

What have I done?

I ignore the blood that's running down my face and let a million scenarios flash through my head. I know exactly how I could put him on his knees. What an accomplishment that would feel like right now; to use everything Brock and Denny have taught me to incapacitate the sick fuck currently standing in front of me. I know exactly how I could do it. I know exactly where to hit, what to keep pressure on, and what to do should he try to get back up.

I know I could take him.

I could get him in the position I am now.

But at what cost?

What will happen if I get him down? Will I be in here longer than four days? Will he spin the story around and try to point the finger at me? Who the fuck would believe me if that happened, especially if Braumer or Becker is paying this guy?

I might get a few guards to side with me. Or maybe one; the kinder woman who registered me into this god-awful fucking place where I don't belong.

7

I hear the zipper on his pants being lowered, so I think fast and grab onto what I hope is the best idea since I came down here. I clear my throat before speaking, keeping my head low, but making sure my eyes catch his actions.

"So, they only want pictures of you beating me? Not forcing yourself on me?"

He slows his movements but doesn't stop. His hand still remains firm on my shoulder when he says, "I got paid. That's all that matters."

I try to calm myself, keep him talking.

"And here I thought they would have paid you bigger money for something like this. Especially Becker," I say.

"I don't ask names, inmate. Not my problem."

I nod my head slowly. "Smart, I suppose. Especially when dealing with the mayor of Chicago. That guy probably has more money than he knows what to do with. Here I thought he would've got a kick out of this and offered you a fortune. Certainly helps him in getting what he wants and keeping his name out of the dirt."

He shakes his head, not at all interested in what I have to say. "Mayor, judge, I don't give a fuck who it is. I'd do this for free princess. Just makes it that much sweeter when I get to keep the photos for later. Sometimes I take videos, but usually I keep those for myself."

The sick bastard smiles down at me. I can barely see it. The light illuminating him from behind gives him a good view of my face but gives me little of his.

I am somewhat getting what I need, and I urge him along. I force myself to soften my voice further and play the innocent inmate, all the while shaking under my skin, ignoring the harsh concrete under my knees.

"Then just hurry up and tape it please. I just want out of here. I want to go home. Just tape it and get it over with, I just want this over!"

I don't need to try hard to keep the tremble in my voice. I am very much afraid at what will become of me when this is over. He did not once imply that I was correct in my assumption that Becker is behind this, nor did he confirm that he wanted this videotaped. He told me our photo shoot was 'over'. So, it's safe to assume that Becker did not want any of this extra shit to happen.

Still, I thank the universe when he pulls out his phone and presses a few buttons. I can only hope that the evidence will get me out of here. Seeming content, he holds the phone in his mouth while he uses the other to pull out his sorry excuse for a cock.

I try to keep the convulsions away, but I can't help it., I lack sleep, and I still have blood dripping from my nose and forehead.

The guard pulls his phone out of his mouth. "Now take it, 76413. You don't get a name down here, just a number. So, show me how much you want to get out of here." He grins, "And make it good."

I whimper a little, playing off the weak woman he wants me to be. He doesn't know me at all. If he did, he would know that weak is the last fucking word you will ever use to describe a beat up, hard, and lonely bitch such as myself. None the less, I play the part.

"Please, I'll be good. I just want to get out of here. Don't hit me anymore, please."

The light from the cell phone beaming down on me confirms that he does, in fact, have the video rolling. I try to prepare myself for what feels more shameful than killing Andrew, but I'm not fast enough. His hand leaves the pressure point on my shoulder to grab the bottom of my jaw, squeezing hard enough that it forces my mouth open.

"Take it, or I'll fucking keep you down here."

I take one last breath through my nose, before he forces himself into my mouth. I ignore the urge to vomit, focusing instead on the light of the camera, opposed to what is in my mouth. I haven't done anything to warrant the sound of pleasure coming from his mouth. I have yet to move any part of my body, especially my tongue.

I won't give him the satisfaction. I remain focused and I keep eye contact before I bite down…As hard as I fucking can.

"AAARRRGHHHH!" The wail coming from his mouth gives me the same amount of sick pleasure as when I heard the same agonizing cries from Andrew. His hand squeezes even tighter on my jaw in an attempt to remove my teeth from his dick, but I can see he's afraid I might take it with me if he pulls back.

"ARRGGHH YOU C-C-CUNT!"

The coppery tang of blood fills my mouth, and only when the skin of his flaccid cock long passes my teeth and hits my gums do, I finally let go.

The guard, who's name I don't know, staggers backward, causing a loud clang when he stumbles into the metal door. He's shaking much like I was a few short moments ago; his hands are now covered in blood as he slumps down to the floor. A mixture of shock, and perhaps blood loss, causing his eyes to roll back in his head.

His cell phone dropped from his hands. I waste no time getting to my feet. I replay Brock's words as I stand in front of him. 'Never stay down, Elle. You get back up, you keep fucking going. The longer you're down, the better chance he has at keeping you there. Don't give him that chance, Elle. You fight, *until you can't fucking stand anymore. When that's done, you fucking fight some more. And when you think it's over? Run, babe. Run as fast as you fucking can.'*

I don't waste time. I look at the amount of blood dripping from the guard, hoping to hell he passes out soon but not counting on it. I swing my arm forward, making contact with his sternum, and follow it with another quick jab to the side of his neck, and lastly his nose. The combination of blows to his pressure points finally makes him pass out.

Knowing I don't have much time, I grab the phone off of the floor, and the radio from the side of his belt. I know I could get his keys and run to get help; but if I'm found running through the hallway, the other guards may get the wrong idea. I pick up the phone, taking a screen shot of the recent call list, and another photo of my face. With shaking fingers, I attach the video and photos quickly, and send them via text to Ryder and Denny's phones. Hoping one of them gets it soon and sends help.

I delete the trace of me sending the video and toss the phone to the other side of the room. I study the radio, noting the sticker on the back. It lists the channels used for each block, and I change it to 0-1 for the emergency channel. I take a few deep breaths, and make sure the guard is still passed out before I bring the radio to my mouth.

"Help, p-p-p-please help me."

I wait a few moments, and a woman's voice comes over the radio waves.

"Lanie, is that you?"

I'm assuming Lanie must be one of the other guards. I'm quick to correct her in the shakiest, weakest voice I can muster.

"N-n-no. P-p-p-please! He's hurting me."
She is fast on the heels of my response. "Where are you?"
she asks.

I sniffle a little, not at all wanting to cry. There are no tears
falling from my eyes, but I do my best to imitate them through
the radio. "I n-n-noticed the le-le-letter 'B'. It-it's d-da-dark."

For once, what sounds like true concern enters the
woman's voice. "B-Block is not occupied, but I'm sending
someone now. Who am I speaking with?"

I curse the bastard in front of me, hating the 'B', hating the
fucking basement, hating the concrete, and hating this cold
fucking place. I do my best to keep up the stutter, and to keep
the anger out of my voice. I decide my best option is to
whisper, saying my given names for the first time in almost a
year.

"J-Jayne. Jayne Elle O'Connor."

I hear the thunder of footsteps above, and I drop the radio.
Whoever is on the other end of it is ignored as I curl myself in
the fetal position on the cold hard floor. I allow the numb to
set in, but this time I absorb it from the concrete beneath me,
not from my heart.

Shock begins to take over as I close my eyes against the
light now coming brighter from the hallway. I see shadows
moving toward me before the blackness starts to set in. It starts
around the outer edges of my vision, moving inward until I see
nothing but black boots in front of my face and a warm hand
touching my arm. It's feminine, and firm.

Only then do I allow the darkness to take me.

Chapter One

Ryder—Two days ago

Becker once again holds the phone out in front of me, and it takes all Denny and Ivan have to hold me back. She has more blood on her beautiful face. There's a large hand wrapped around her hair to hold her head up, and her fucking shirt is torn.

Hang on beautiful! Don't let go, just hang the fuck on!

"Noon tomorrow, Mr. Callaghan. If you're not there, I can assure you that you will regret it."

I leap forward, hoping to strangle the smug son of a bitch but Denny grabs me by my arm. I barely get another step forward before the car is speeding off down the street, taking the contact between me and the only woman I have ever given two fucks about.

I pull from Denny's grasp, putting my head in my hands and pulling on my hair.

"Jesus, fuck! Fuck! Ivan? Where the fuck is Ivan? Get Patrov on the phone. Get her out of that fucking place…"

Strong hands clamp down on my shoulders, half pulling me back up. "Petrov is on his way, he's calling in a few favors as we speak. Let's take this inside, boss."

Annoyed, yet thankful for Denny's level headedness, I do as I am told for the first fucking time in my life and storm toward Jimmy's shop. He's oddly silent but won't stay still. This has to be hurting him as much as it is hurting me.

What the fuck was I thinking? How the fuck did I bring such a beautiful fucking woman into this mess?

What the hell am I going to do?

Denny shoves a phone into my face, and I note the name before I put it to my ear. "Andrei, if anything else happens to my woman, there won't be a goddamn thing anyone can do to stop me. So help me fucking god, if I see one more drop of blood run down Elle's face…"

"Ryder, listen!" He says firmly, "I have two contacts in the facility. Unfortunately, neither of them have been assigned to the block that Jay—*Elle's* being held. I have contacted them both and they are going to look into it for me, *immediately*. If something more happens to her I can guarantee you that I will have the person who's responsible killed myself. *That* is a promise. Now, sit tight for ten fucking minutes and we'll talk about this face to face."

I hang up the phone on the thickly accented Russian man and toss is back to Denny. I want nothing more than to beat the living fuck out of someone, but I sense the tension coming off Jimmy and begin to worry who he feels like beating on. We're men, it's what we do. Beat on shit and take out our frustration; most of the time not giving two fucks who it was who got the beating, so long as we feel better afterward.

I take the twenty steps across the shop toward him. I open my mouth to let him know what's going on, but don't get a word out before his fist slams me in the jaw with enough force that I stumble into the table.

I don't move to hit him back, but fuck do I want to. I regain my footing and he wastes no time pointing his finger in my face to let me know exactly how he feels.

"You son of a bitch! You better be ready for this!"

I don't know what he's referring to, but he clears it up for me. "You want to know who fucking held her when her family died? I did! You want to know who forced her to fucking eat and then spiked her wine with sleeping pills so she could fucking *sleep*? I did! I watched my best friend fall the fuck apart and stare out a goddamn window like a crazy person for months!

"Laura had to force her into the goddamn shower while I crushed Jay's pills. Not once, but *twice*, because life couldn't just hand her one shit hand by stealing her fucking family." He barks out a harsh laugh with no humor, "No! It had to hand another one to the best fucking woman I know when she was beat and fucking tortured to near death a second time! So, I stood, in her fucking kitchen, preparing her nightly cocktail to make sure that the only good woman left in my life got to fucking sleep!

"I did everything short of wiping her ass, Callaghan! All because she was falling apart. She wouldn't ask for help, she wouldn't talk. She wouldn't do a goddamn thing! She just fucking sat there, *useless*. Ignorant to everything that was going on around her."

His fingers thread into his short hair, "I'm not an idiot and I understand that this shit going on right now is out of our control. But I'll tell you right now Ryder, I finally got a small glimpse of the woman she used to be when she came back here. She's hard, she's rough, but she is still and will always be the most beautiful fucking woman in my life.

"That said, if she breaks this time?" He points at me, "It's on you. I am telling you right now that if you can't handle that, if you can't handle a mute who is going to ignore you, shut you out and almost forget you, then walk away now. Leave, and don't fucking come back. I've lost her twice. I will do it again until the day I die because she is the only family I have, and I love her to death. But don't give her anymore hope. Because if you can't handle it, the way she is going to be when she gets out—I will kill you. I am telling you now, she will break even more if you can't put up with it. That's assuming she makes it out of this fucked up mess alive and half-sane."

I wipe the blood from my mouth, ignoring the burn in my jaw. Jimmy is not as big as I am, but he packs one hell of a punch. He also cares about my stubborn woman more than I care to let on.

Am I happy she's had him in her life? Absolutely. Everybody needs someone who cares for them. But I will make it my fucking mission to let him and her know that she's my responsibility.

She's mine to look after.

She's mine to hold at night, to keep her nightmares away.

She's just fucking *mine*.

"Hit me again Jimmy, hit me as many times as you want. I deserve it, I know I do. I should've done better to keep this shit from touching her but trust me when I say that I'm not going anywhere. I'm not leaving because I…"

I take a deep breath, closing my eyes for a moment.

We're both silent until he breaks it. "You love her," he says. Not as a question, but as a statement.

I look into the eyes of my life's best friend, and simply nod my head. I haven't said it out loud…but that's for her, not him.

I love her.

Jimmy seems satisfied with my non-verbal answer, because he extends his hand. I grasp it firmly to shake, acknowledging our silent agreement.

Elle is mine.

I will look after her; I will never leave her. No matter what happens, I will stand by that woman's side and make sure she comes out of this intact. She means that much to me. She means everything to me. I was just too fucking dumb to admit or do something about it.

No more.

Never again.

She'll know and I'll remind her every fucking day.

"Boss, Petrov is here."

I let go of Jimmy's hand and greet a surprisingly irate Andrei Petrov as he enters Jimmy's shop. "Not my fucking idea of Friday night, gentlemen. Sit down, let's go over what we know, and what we can do."

I don't for one second disrespect a man like Andrei Petrov. Me and my team are some badass motherfuckers, and I lost it with him earlier—most likely will again. But that doesn't mean my attitude didn't come from a good place. I know he knows that, so I don't bother apologizing.

I never agreed with a few of the men he got off on murder charges in the past. Hell, some of them I would kill myself before setting them free on the streets. But right now? I need him.

I hate to admit that my hands are tied.

If this happened back home? I'd be golden. I know enough people in law enforcement and the court system to be able to keep my woman out of this mess. In Canada? I have no fucking pull other than a few men I happened to meet while I served overseas.

Reluctantly, I take my seat at the table Jimmy has set up in the shop. He obviously uses it to sit and make sketches, go over plans with clients, etc. It's a huge, dark oak number, classically aged with cigarette burn marks and faded ring marks from drinks.

I motion to his pack on the table and he pushes it my way. I light one up before I toss it back to him. I relish in the burn as it makes its way into my once healthy lungs. On my exhale, I note all eyes on me. Everyone is waiting for me to lock my shit down before they begin.

I look to Jimmy, giving him the respect he deserves. He is as much a part of this as I am. I hate to admit it, but maybe more so. He's been with Elle longer than I have. I may have been the one to get Elle into this mess, but it has been him and her friend Laura who got her out of it before and brought her back to life. I made a silent vow when I shook hands with Jimmy, and I won't let him down. I will stand by that woman from now until the day I die, making sure she has everything she needs and anything she might want.

Jimmy nods back to me, thankful for the support and appreciation. I nod toward Petrov who wastes no time getting to the point.

"One of my contacts at the prison got back to me. She is being held in Block-D, which is not where my contact is located but she assures me she was in her cell for check-in almost an hour ago. I have a list of the guards on duty tonight, and I am certain I know which one is responsible for what happened.

"His name is Derek Stratus; and this would not be the first complaint. Something you have to remember is the prison sees a lot of women who are not like our Jayne, or *Elle*."

Andrei shoots me a sympathetic expression before he continues. "This place has everything from women who have molested children, to killers. They also have your run of the mill drug dealers and junkies. It's unfortunate this is where she is, but it was the closest facility to the courthouse.

"All of that aside, Stratus has a bad rap, but he gets away with it because the type of women who usually make complaints against him are not reputable. My contacts have told me so and I have heard it through other sources. My contact is currently trying to track her down, but I got a text when I arrived that reads she is not in her cell on D-Block."

I slam my fist against the table, at the same moment Jimmy shoots out of his chair and lets loose a string of profanity.

"What the fuck do we do, Petrov? Because I am telling you right now that I am this fucking close to burning down the home of the goddamn judge who sent her there in the first place!"

He makes a motion of surrender with his hands before continuing. "I will be the first to issue a hit on the sick fuck who is doing this, I promise you. Right now, I need you to wait like I am for my contact to get back to me. We can't break down the prison to find her, and we can do nothing until court resumes on Tuesday other than use my contacts on the inside. Please, trust me when I say that they will not let me down."

I run my hands down my face and through my hair, knowing by the look on Petrov's face that he is absolutely serious. There are few people in this world who would not do their damndest to make sure they got him the answers he wanted, and *fast*. But that doesn't negate the fact I have a hard time putting my trust into people who I don't know. It also doesn't mean it's not frustrating as fuck sitting here waiting. I just want answers! I don't want to wait, and as much as I know Petrov will do what he can to help, I need to know how far that help will go. So I ask him, "Petrov, you know I'm grateful that you're here, but fucking forgive me if I can't take someone's word right now. My goddamn woman is being beaten and possibly raped at the moment, and you ask me to just sit with my fucking thumb up my ass and put my trust in someone I've never met? Give me something more Andrei, I don't care what it costs just fucking give me something!"

Andrei Petrov, smug fucker that he is, replies with a smirk and a sense of pride on his face. "Do you remember Gerald D. Cordova? He was once held at the same prison that Elle is at now—in the men's wing, of course."

I take stock of the information in my head, the name sounds familiar but it doesn't ring any immediate bells. Denny clears up my confusion, clearing his throat before he speaks, staring at the wall.

"Long-time child molester, rapist, and killer. Originally from Toronto, but was a repeat offender in the United States and across Canada."

I see the hurt in my friend's eyes, understanding his sensitivity on the subject after what he went through with Grace. Petrov's Russian accent pulls me from my thoughts. "Ah, yes. I believe you read that he escaped transport, only for his decomposed body to be found a few years later in the river. What you did not hear, however, is how my contacts allowed him to be taken from the transport so that one of the victim's fathers could torture him for twenty-four hours. Usually I take money for these types of transactions, however sometimes I feel the need to be philanthropic and take pleasure in doing it for free." Then the crazy prick smiles like the cat who ate the canary.

I stare at the man who is defending my woman, having nothing but respect for him after what he just told me. Some might call me a sadist but inflicting pain is something I was good at when it came to interrogation, and I take pleasure when I know the fucker on the other side of my torture thoroughly fucking deserved it.

I know a bit about some of the men he has defended in the past. I also know about the men they have killed. People in the media don't hold a candle for Petrov, but I know for a fact the men who were killed on behalf of some of his clients deserved what they got. I also know the men did other shit that warranted keeping them there.

Petrov is not a bad guy, per se. He's the kind of man you want on your good side when shit goes south and you need to step slightly outside the lines of the law in order to get justice.

"The sick fuck deserved what he got Andrei, but I just need to know that Elle is okay."

Like a prayer answered, Andrei's phone rings. I jump from my chair, prepared to stand beside him and listen in to the conversation if I need to. I don't care how much it makes me look like a fucking pussy—I need to know that she's alright.

"Speaker," Ivan says.

Andrei nods and answers his phone, placing it on the table. "Marnie, how's my client?"

A woman, who I am assuming either works a desk or as a guard, answers Andrei. "I only have a few seconds. She's a mess, she's unconscious and they're sending her to the infirmary."

I grab an empty beer bottle from the table and throw it against the nearest wall. At the same time, Jimmy knocks over another chair and starts pacing around the table looking for something to punch.

"Marnie, I need details, please."

I hear some shuffling on the other end of the line. "Jesus Andrei, I'm going to lose my fuckin' job. Listen, the woman is fine. She's beat up, but she's okay. If I were her I would have passed the fuck out too. She's going to have some bumps and bruises—shit—she might even need therapy. But let me tell you; never in my fifteen years of workin' here have I seen anything like it. That is one tough bitch you got, Andrei."

Andrei moves to speak into the phone but I cut him off, needing to know more. "Tell me. That's my woman! Just fucking tell me what happened. Please!"

"Andrei, you know I don't like speaking to anyone but you, if I lose my job you bet your ass you're paying for my retirement!" she says in an angry voice. Andrei gives me a scolding look before placating Marnie.

"Marnie, he's not a civilian. Think of someone like Rambo, or G.I Joe." He jokes, "Trust me, he is okay. Now tell us please.".

"Jesus, listen; I know who that woman is, read the story about her in the papers. Like I said, one tough bitch. The girl not only got him down, but he'll be lucky if he ever gets his dick up again. I told you—never seen anything like it!"

Andrei lets out an annoyed huff. "Like what Marnie, details!"

Her raised voice comes through the speaker. "His pants were around his ankles and there was more blood than when I gave birth to my first child. She tried to bite his fuckin' dick off, Andrei! And if she bit down another hair's width I'm sure she would have succeeded! Prick would be lucky if he gets it up again!"

I don't miss the small look of satisfaction on all the men's faces. Denny, Jimmy Ivan and Andrei. I miss the same look because I'm fuming that some sick fuck tried to violate my woman and shoved his cock into her sweet mouth.

That's *my* mouth.

Marnie presses on while I reach in my pocket for my phone, preparing to call my contact at The Tribune in Chicago. Becker's games are over. Fuck him and Foley. This shit ends now.

I let Marnie's words filter in my ears as I open my phone. "I need to get back, this only happened not ten minutes ago and I'm behind on my rounds. I'll call if anything comes up. Gotta go."

"Holy fuck, boss! "I too, am experiencing the same sentiment as Denny as I look at my phone.

"No! Fuck NO!" I see the picture before I see the link to the video. I hear the commotion around me, but focus on the photo with phone numbers, one being a Chicago area code. I see Jimmy out of my peripheral vision swiping something on Denny's phone before the image comes to life on the TV in the shop. I take my eyes off my own phone as I see the same video still on the television.

"It has the same area code as Elle's burner. Becker didn't send this," Ivan says.

"It's ours, press play Denny," says Jimmy.

I'm not at all prepared for what I am about to witness. Nor are my men. Ivan clamps a hand down on my shoulder, and I stand, stunned fucking stupid and ready to shed blood.

"Now take it, 76413. You don't get a name down here, just a number. So show me how much you want to get out of here. And make it good."

My beautiful woman whimpers, clearly fucking helpless and distraught with what this bastard wants her to do. I see her blood-stained face, and some filthy fuck's hand on her shoulder holding her down.

"Please, I'll be good. I just want to get out of here. Don't hit me anymore, please."

I listen to my girl's voice, trying to make sense of an emotion I haven't heard before when Jimmy cuts off my train of thought.

"That's not Jay, she's playing him."

He cuts himself short to finish watching the awful shit playing in front of us. Elle barely finished speaking before the prick grabs her by the jaw, forcing her mouth open.

"Take it, or I'll fucking keep you down here."

I'm two steps away from tearing Jimmy's smart TV off the wall, before I become the proudest fucking man in the history of mankind. Hoots and hollers surround me as I watch my beautiful, smart fucking woman. I should have known what Jimmy did, those scared eyes and that meek voice is not my cold-hearted woman. She won't cave, and she would never back down. I feel sick to my stomach for thinking so little of her, assuming she couldn't handle herself in a place like that.

Always wanting to protect her.

I don't hide the surge of pride that I feel as I watch her bite down on the sorry excuse this man calls a cock. I also take sick pleasure listening to the howl coming from the guard's mouth.

He'll howl like that again; I'll make sure of it.

I watch the evil in my woman's eyes when she doesn't let go. I want to wash that hate and fury out of those beautiful greens but I know it's what's keeping her alive right now. She won't break yet. She'll hold onto the hate before she allows herself to feel pain. I see the blood running from her mouth and the sick satisfaction on her face before the phone falls to the floor, the video feed lost.

I noticed the time stamp, letting us know it happened no less than thirty minutes ago. I no sooner blink my eyes before Andrei's phone begins to ring.

"She's with the medic now. She'll be safe there."

I breathe the first sigh of relief in what feels like months, knowing that someone is helping to look after my Elle. I see the last photo she sent; blood running down her face from the beating she took. And blood running out of her mouth from the damage her teeth caused.

I love you, beautiful, and I'm proud of you. Just hang the fuck on.

Chapter Two

Elle

I think back to the song I sang for Ryder. Not to him directly of course, but to the concrete walls in the prison.

Bite your tongue,
Don't make a scene dear.
Everybody's been here,
At least once before;
But we've been here more.

I made a scene. I also bit down on something that was most certainly not my tongue. And to sum it all up, I have been here before. The déjà vu set in, and is wound so tight you would have sworn rigor mortis had set in as well. I'm not sure how I get myself into these situations. I'm not even sure if perhaps I deserve it or not.

So I stare at the bland, beige walls in the prison infirmary. I don't hate the beige; it's better than cold and bare concrete so I'll take painted walls with windows any day of the week, in whatever fucking color you want to paint them.

I'm not sure how long I've been laying here. I want to say I blacked out but that's not true because I remember everything from the time they peeled me off the floor in B-Block to the time they brought me up here. They assumed I was unconscious but for me it was like playing dead. I stayed mute and unfocused as they hefted me up and put me on a stretcher. Now, I just feel like my mind is here but my body is gone, or perhaps it's vice versa.

I don't know.

But this is different because I really don't *feel* it. Everything is completely numb. I knew I needed to embrace the woman I was months ago—pre-Ryder. I also knew I needed to remember everything Brock and Denny had taught me in order to get out alive. I still don't fear death like I once did, but I'll be damned if I go out letting someone take advantage of me.

I'm not sure what it was but something happened to me in B-Block, something that didn't happen the last time I fought back. I'm not sure why this time is any different but the only thing I can think of is *I've been here before.*

I've been in this bed, with bandages on my face.

I've been beat down, slightly broken and used up.

I've been in this room, which stinks of latex and antiseptic.

I've been here before.

I am by no means in the poor shape I once was. Not on the outside anyway. I haven't moved my body in hours but I know nothing is broken. I also know that only five stitches were sewn into my purchased face.

The nurse was not mean to me, nor was the doctor. They were straight and to the point. They asked me if I thought anything else was wrong with me besides what was visible, to which I shook my head in the negative.

They asked me if I was sexually assaulted to which I also shook my head in the negative, after the doctor's eyes motioned to my lower half. After cleaning my face up and giving me a new clean, nondescript cotton shirt, much the same as the one I had on, they stitched up my face. The final question was if I needed any pain medication or wished to talk to a counselor, to which I once again shook my head.

I have not spoken, nor do I intend to.

I'm done with people. Or at least the people in here. I played my part; I was kind, I did not act out in any way, nor did I give anyone the excuse to treat me poorly.

Yet here I am.

Of course it's not entirely the fault of the people here, I know Becker had to have pulled some of those strings. I also know that Braumer most likely has that sick, god awful smirk on his face. The one I plan to remove at my earliest convenience.

The fat fuck wouldn't even see it coming—he sure as shit deserves it too.

So here I lie; staring at the wall refusing to close my eyes, and waiting.

For what? I don't know.

I just know that something is coming.

And it's going be big.

* * *

Ryder

I've paced these floors since last night when the video came in. I haven't slept, nor do I want to.

I'm waiting.

I haven't heard much else from Andrei's contacts. Or I guess I should say *we* haven't, but it means little to me. All I know is that she's still in the infirmary; they assume she's in shock, but other than that she's safe.

Andrei made arrangements with his contact to find more good people in the prison to look after Elle. He knew two before, but that's not enough for when shift change rolls around. I also know that the fucker whose dick she near bit off—*Stratus*—was shipped to the men's wing of the prison to be looked after, and when there wasn't anything they could do for him there, he was transported to a nearby hospital which was better equipped to sew his sorry cock back together.

I look at the clock. 11:59 a.m.

My men watch as I press a few buttons on my phone to make the call. If there's any victory made in the last twelve hours, this is it. I knew I couldn't call him last night; he'd be on a plane. I listen to it ring before his haughty voice comes on the line.

"Callaghan, I'm assuming you're arranging a time to meet? I must say I'm surprised, I figured you would be greeting me at my office."

I take a deep breath, reveling in the fact that this should be the last time I ever speak to this fucking prick again. "The Chicago Tribune gets a lot of online readers. The reason I'm telling you this is because today's paper gets set to print the night before so it was a little hard to get the story in on time."

I hear the prick huff on the other end of the line before he says, "Ryder, really? We're back to this? One phone call and…" I cut him off. "And nothing! Your time's up Becker. I'm guessing right about now those lights on your phone are going to start lighting up along with your reputation. Albeit not in a good way, in a go down in fucking flames sort of way.

"I told you I don't do well when people fuck with me or my woman, and this is where we are. The reason all those lights

29

are flashing is because The Tribune, along with the Daily Post, are running a *nooner* Becker. And by *nooner* I don't just mean the ones you partook in with the overpriced pussy from Tenth Avenue; I mean it's an online exclusive that was set to release while all of your Armani wearing, gavel rearing, golf club sporting pricks could enjoy it over a single malt while eating lunch at The Regency."

I hear commotion in the background, his office door opening, and his too-young-to-be-fucked-by-the-old-bastard's secretary harping in the distance.

"You're done," he says in a gruff voice.

"No Becker. You are."

I hang up the phone and stuff it my pocket.

I know he bought the judge on Elle's case, but there's no paper trail yet so I can't prove it. Either way that judge would be extremely fucking stupid to take on a favor from a ruined Mayor at this point.

Becker's out of the game.

Now I gotta get my girl.

Chapter Three

Elle—Present day

I hear the door opening and closing but I rarely look at who comes in. I know their footsteps now. I've been lying in this bed for what feels like days. I've gotten up to go to the bathroom because never again in my life do I wish to piss myself. But aside from that venture, that's it.

They put an IV in my arm because I refused to eat. Not because I don't need food but because I don't want anything else in my mouth. I feel like I would be sick if I tried to eat anything so I don't bother, not yet anyway.

Since I know their footsteps, I know that along with the nurse, who I've labeled 'Susan' because she looks like a Susan, there is someone else with her. I don't turn around, nor do I look away from the wall when I see the Armani suit pants and Italian leather shoes come into my line of sight. I also know who it is because I remember his cologne. It's nice, understated.

A chair is pulled up and he tugs on his pant legs before he takes a seat, putting his face level with mine.

Andrei Patrov studies me. I watch the lines between his eyebrows appear—a sign of his dissatisfaction at what has become of me. I also watch as something that wouldn't be described as pity but more like appreciation crosses his face.

In a low voice he says, "I cannot say that I have ever met a woman such as you. What I can say is that not only am I fascinated by what you can do in a dire situation, I am inspired by you."

I'm mildly surprised by Andrei's words, and I don't get a chance to reflect before he continues.

"I will not lie to you and say that I see women as strong creatures; because for the better part of my life I have seen weak ones. In my eyes and in my experience, women are to be looked after and cared for, never allowing them a moment to break a nail or harm a hair on their head. I am dominant by nature, but that does not mean that I do not respect those who deserve it.

"That being said, you have given me a whole new perspective. You, for lack of a better term are a fighter, Jayne. And I promise you I will fight just as hard to look after you. I also promise many other things which cannot be discussed in the room because I cannot guarantee that it is secure."

He leans close, gaining my eye contact, saying no words. I know what he means so I give him a small gesture with a head movement.

"I will see you out of here. I promise you this."

His accent is thick and I don't mistake the gruffness. He's at his end with patience and I know that justice will be served.

Outside the law.

* * *

Denny

I watch Bonnie MacIntosh, the woman responsible for putting Elle in jail, leave her apartment for the tenth time in the past few days.

I guess I shouldn't call her responsible. It was Braumer who paid her, but it was most likely Becker who footed the bill in the first place. Either way, she's in and out a lot today. It started last night when she left for work at a local coffee shop where she waits tables. She got in around eleven last night and left again this morning at seven to head to a mom and pop breakfast place where she also waits tables.

I've been watching her on and off for three days now, alternating shifts with Ivan. It's not as exciting as some of the other jobs we've been on but she's not hard to look at. She's a petite woman. From the info Cabe gave me, her medical file, I know she's five-foot-four and roughly 120 lbs. She's healthy; no record of drug use although she's been charged for possession.

She's had six jobs in the past fourteen months and seems to spend every moment she can with her two-year-old son. She has long russet hair and olive skin. Most likely, she has a bit of Italian in her. Those big, sky-blue eyes suggest that one of her parents is not at all Italian but maybe Irish.

She has a small nose and high cheekbones.

She's beautiful.

I wouldn't have called her that three days ago because even I know ugly lies beneath a shiny exterior. But something is amiss here. This woman is not a bad person, nor would she harm anyone. I watched her help an elderly woman carry her groceries into the building. I also watched her at work while she smiled and goofed off with a few young children at one of her tables.

I haven't seen Braumer or any of Becker's men approach her. I'm also fucking good at what I do so I know I didn't miss anything. I could miss a phone call but that's being taken care of on Cabe's end. If she called or got a call, we would know about it. So far it's only been from her place of work, and an out of province call, which we figured out was a family member.

I grab my vibrating phone out of the cup holder and answer Ryder's call.

"Boss?"

He hates when we greet him that way but that's what he is so we don't stop. Ryder treats us all like brothers, family. So he has a hard time getting used to it.

"Time to move. Court is less than twenty-four hours out. Break her down and get some answers. But do it quietly, Denny."

"Ten-four, boss."

I hang up my phone to extract my orders. Bonnie's roommate works eight to four. It's only eleven. I have five hours to get my answers from the woman with the sky-blue eyes.

I won't fail.

Chapter Four

Ryder

"It's been thirty-six hours Patrov! Thirty-six!"

He leans across Jimmy's table, the one we sat around two nights ago when the video came in. He's more relaxed than I like to see and that pisses me the fuck off. I haven't slept, I've barely eaten. I've paced this shop from top to bottom and back again. It's not often that I lose my shit.

Correction, I never lose my shit.

But I've never cared for someone as much as I do Elle, and I'm having one fuck of a time trying to keep my shit checked.

"Callaghan, she's safe. That's all that matters because at this point, as well as thirty-six hours ago, it is the only thing we can hope for. I'm here because we need to go over a few things before we get to court."

I can't help my attitude. And no matter how many times he tells me she's safe, I won't feel the same way until she's here, in my arms.

"First off, we need to speak with Denny. Ivan said he shook Bonnie Macintosh, I know he knows that she was paid but I need to know if she put it in writing."

I have enough balls to eyeball Patrov. I'm not a stupid fucker and I've worked this game before. "It's solid Patrov. But there's still a screw or two loose in the foundation because we haven't seen Braumer, nor do we know if the judge will approve of her recanting her statement."

"Ryder, all I need to know is if she dropped pressing charges. If she does that, we'll be okay. It's one last nail in the coffin when we walk in there today."

I nod my head in understanding. "She's dropping them, but she's also scared shitless that Braumer is going to come after her. She was assured that with Becker out the picture, Braumer doesn't have the money to keep her where she is. Anyway, I don't know all the small, shit details. Denny's looking after it and Ivan is out looking for Braumer. Both will meet us at the courthouse to be there for Elle."

I see a small amount of apprehension cross his face before he locks it down and nods. My guys want to be there for Elle almost as much as I do. They respect her and they'll show her that respect by standing behind her today.

"Alright, with that all aside, I'm heading over to the courthouse because I have a few people I want to talk to. In the meantime, Callaghan, go eat and shower. You can't help her if you can't help yourself. I say this with respect; look after you so you can look after her."

I'm two seconds away from saying something I may regret, and trust me, I regret little in my life. But I know he's right. I've avoided sleep food and the bathroom in favor of pacing this garage and keeping my phone plugged into the wall.

I settle for a chin lift in acknowledgment before doing just so.

After, I'll go get my woman.

Chapter Five

Elle

The ride in the back of the police cruiser is quiet. I don't know the officer escorting me and he doesn't say much, but I do as he and the rookie woman officer says. I don't act out of line, I don't talk back.

I don't like travelling in handcuffs. In fact, I don't like handcuffs at all. I remember thinking about all the things that could be done with them. In the bedroom that is. For most of us it's a complete turn on but for me, being on the other side of these when they're used in a non-consensual way—well let's just say it won't be my cup of tea.

I'm in desperate need of a good shower. I was thankful that while in the infirmary the shower was rather private. I didn't get a razor or nice conditioner to use though. Needless to say, my leg hair is four days long and my hair is in its usual bird's nest with a lot more fuzz seeing as I didn't have any product to tame it.

I found an elastic band on the desk when I was being escorted out. I motioned to it and the woman on the other side allowed me to take it. With my hands cuffed, I did the best messy bun I could and called it better than a bird's nest for court.

I got to change back into my pre-prison clothes. So on top of the no shaving, I have on the same underwear I wore four days ago. Life could be worse so I don't dwell on it. A few days ago I was forced to my knees, so I'm not going to complain about dirty undergarments.

We pull in to the entrance of the underground garage. There are two security guards who check the officers' IDs, as well as ogle me in the back seat before we are allowed entry. From there it's a reverse repeat of last time.

Get out of the car, walk to the elevator. Exit the elevator and move to the room Andrei is assigned. My cuffs are removed, thank god, and the guards leave me with him to have a few words before the hearing.

Little is said between the two of us. He tells me that Bonnie is dropping the charges and little else. Seeing as I'm not allowed to speak unless spoken to when I get in there, I don't put up a fuss. He's not telling me to lie about anything, he's not telling me to say anything at all so I assume I won't need to speak.

We exit the room through a different door and enter the courtroom. Andrei is ahead of me and I'm escorted with an officer at my side. I try not to because I don't want to crack my armor, but I can't help but search for Ryder. I use search as a loose term because he's impossible to miss. Today he's wearing an impeccable suit. And despite my earlier emotion of not being able to feel anything, I know he looks fucking good in it—it causes a flutter in my stomach.

It's charcoal in color with small pinstripes, and he has a pristine white shirt underneath and a silver-grey tie that reminds me of his eyes. I hate that the suit reminds me of when he went to the fundraiser with Claudia Becker, but I push that thought aside to look at the other handsome men beside him.

Denny is just as dapper, surprising me to say the least that my Viking god of a trainer cleans up so well. He's wearing a dark grey suit but his shirt is black. Unbuttoned at the collar and no tie.

Ivan cleans up just as well, all black and broad shouldered. These intelligent and wonderful men are here to support me. When I'm able to speak again I'll be sure to tell them how grateful I am.

THE UGLY ROSES

Jimmy, Laura and her man Brad flank them to the left. My best friend has tears in her eyes. I can't handle them right now so I skim past her, taking in Jimmy and Brad's clean-cut suits and dress slacks.

I'm not an idiot. These people are my family, and as much as I don't want them to see me in here, I'm glad my back won't feel cold with all of those big empty benches behind me. It will be warmed by the people who continually try to thaw me.

Ryder's eyes carefully watch every movement I make. I know he wants to come to me. I can see the despair in his eyes. Of course, the despair is masked underneath a layer of fury and anguish. None the less, I know that while I've been away he would be doing all that he could to get me back.

That's not just who he is, it's who I am to him.

Andrei leads me to our seats and Ryder's hand reaches out, his fingertips brushing against mine in silent support. It's not enough to make me cry, but it's enough to remind myself that I want more of his touch. The warmth that flows from him to me is undeniable, like the connection we share.

That's the fucked-up thing about being attacked. Last time I wanted nothing to do with touches, but this time I want nothing more than for him to wrap his strong arms around me and hold tight. I'm strong. I've pulled through this and all the other shit I've been through. But for just a little while I want someone to be strong *for* me. I put on my tough front when it's needed, and I will continue to keep that invisible armor in place while I'm here today, but I need to let go. I need to break. Not completely, just enough to let Ryder in, and let some of the hatred and fury out.

I ignore what I want for the time being, settling down into my chair beside my lawyer. We rise briefly when the judge enters the room, but other than that I do what I was told. Sit, stay quiet, only speak when spoken to.

I know I look like hell. The right side of my face is bruised and swollen from my nose to my eye. It opens halfway but I don't push it any further because it hurts the stitches above my eyebrow.

I listen to the beginning of the court proceedings. Hoping my fate is much sweeter than the last time I was here.

"Your honor, I am sure you have been privy to the information regarding what happened to my client while she was being held over the weekend. In light of this fact, I hope we can make today quick and painless as she has endured enough of the latter these past few days."

To my surprise, the judge casts a glance my way nodding his head in the affirmative, and ruffles through some paperwork before he addresses us. "Yes, I heard and should she wish to file charges, she may do so after we are finished here today. Now, in light of the harassment charges against Ms. O'Connor being dropped, and since there is no concrete proof of her aggressive behavior, I don't see a reason for us to drag this out any longer than necessary Mr. Patrov."

"Thank you, your honor."

The judge leans forward, "However, due to the fact that there still seems to be an unsolved case in regard to Mr. Andrew Roberts and Cory Gallagher; I will ask that your client remain close and available should the authorities wish to question her further."

Patrov nods in acceptance. "Of course."

The judge looks to me and I too give him silent agreement. "Very well. You're free to go Ms. O'Connor, court is adjourned."

The gavel no sooner slams then Ryder is at my side. I don't fight it; I welcome the embrace with open arms. He breathes me in and I have no doubt I smell nothing like I did before. The lingering scent of coconut is long gone and replaced with antiseptic. Still he inhales me like a junkie would his next fix.

"Fuck beautiful, I missed you."

I don't get a chance to respond as he pulls my face out of his chest, and moves his large capable hands to either side of my neck. His thumbs brush my jaw so lightly I barely feel it.

"I want to get out of here Ryder."

I plead with my eyes and his black one's blaze something fierce when they look over my slightly battered face. He nods quickly, "let's go."

I move my eyes to Jimmy and Laura, silently asking them to sit this one out, just for a little while. They must sense my un-ease, or perhaps they know my needs better than I do because Jimmy puts his arm around Laura and they nod in acceptance. I reach out and put my hand on Brad's arm, giving it a small squeeze. I haven't seen him in almost a year but that doesn't mean I'm not thankful for him coming today.

He gives me a chin lift, so I drop my hand and allow Ryder to lead me out of the courthouse.

* * *

I'm silent as Ryder pulls me by my hand to a black SUV parked close by. I'm still in a little bit of shock. He reaches across me and buckles my seatbelt when he gets in on the driver's side. I would never *not* wear one, but my mind isn't on autopilot right now. It's just on nothing. I want to go somewhere familiar, have a shower, and sleep for the next two days. In one sense it seems like just yesterday when I was attacked, and in another it feels like a lifetime ago. I need rest before I can put my head back together.

After my belt is secured, Ryder stays leaned over the console. His left hand comes up and brushes some of the hair back off my face. His eyes are pained, like he's discovering the marks on my face for the first time. He seems to shake himself out of it before placing his lips on my forehead. I close my eyes at the contact, grateful for it yet not satisfied because it's not enough.

"I'm gonna get you out of here beautiful, then we'll talk."

I nod my head, not because I want to talk but because I want to get out of here. He seems placated with my nonverbal answer and puts the truck in drive. I stare out the window, watching as life passes me by. I take in the taller buildings around the courthouse, thankful I live outside the city in a smaller township. Well, used to live. But for the moment I want the quiet. Not the hustle and bustle of all the cars around us. The people wandering to a fro about their lives not knowing what kind of evil is truly out there. I briefly think of the fact that I am back here for a reason, and that reason is because I am trying to find out who Andrew's brother is.

I haven't thought about it at all these past four days. I haven't thought about anything other than getting out of jail, and then trying to push what happened with the guard into the deep recesses of my mind.

I know the answer before I ask, but I do it anyway.

"Maverick?"

Last I heard he was still in the bush, waiting for what would hopefully be Andrew's brother to show up at the cabin in Pine Point. Ryder's grip tightens on the steering wheel. "No sign of the brother, beautiful. Mav set up surveillance so he's not sitting there. He rented a cabin two miles out but with the surveillance he'll know if someone shows up."

I nod, not because I like the answer. I am glad he's not directly in harm's way should Andrew's brother show up, I'm just not pleased they still haven't been able to find him.

The rest of the drive is in silence, aside from the radio being on low. I watch the city life turn into small town while listening to the words of Mumford and Sons' *'Believe'* come through the speakers. Music becomes one with me as I listen to the words, hoping that one day I can, in fact, *believe.*

I'm not sure what yet, but just to *believe.*

In *something.*

Anything.

Chapter Six

Ryder punches in the code on the back of Jimmy's building and leads me upstairs. I'm not surprised this is where we arrived. I do feel differently when he leads me to the spare room. I take note of the bag in the corner, and Ryder's black boots sitting next to it.

He stayed here while I was gone.

Norma comes barreling out of Jimmy's room with a huge smile on her face as she plants her big behind at my feet, waiting for love. I lean down and embrace my beautiful girl, running my hands over her silky fur, letting her know that I missed her and she was not forgotten.

Ryder removes his suit jacket. His belt shoes and socks go next and then he grabs my hand to lead me toward the bathroom. It's like he's taking over my autopilot for me. He turns the shower on then turns back to me and begins undoing the buttons on his shirt. One by one they open to reveal his tanned skin and black ink before it's completely off and hanging on the back of the bathroom door.

Taking one step closer, his hands reach up and untangle the rubber office supply elastic from my hair. It falls around my face and shoulders. He pushes it back, keeping my face visible.

Strong but gentle hands reach for the bottom of my shirt while his eyes come to mine, seeking permission. I raise my arms above my head and the grey tunic top is gently taken off. He kneels in front of me, removing my sandals and setting them aside. His hands go to my waist next and he lowers my black tights, taking the underwear I wore four days ago with them.

THE UGLY ROSES

I stand in nothing but my bra as he rises to remove that too. I'm not shy in front of him, nor do I move to cover the slight bruising on my side from the concrete floor when I hear him hiss.

I leave my hands at my sides and watch him removing his own dress pants and boxers. Once they're discarded, he puts his hands on my shoulders, running them slowly down my arms until they reach my hands. He entwines our fingers and pulls me forward, lips settling against my forehead as he speaks. "We're going to shower, and if you're hungry after that I'm going to feed you. After, regardless that it's only two in the afternoon, I'm going to take you to bed."

I have no objections whatsoever other than the fact I still don't have an appetite so I shake my head.

"Just shower and bed."

His only answer is to pull me toward the shower. Opening the door, he gets in first, adjusting the temperature before pulling me in behind him. I don't take the time like I normally would to appreciate his backside, nor do I ogle the front of him as the first droplets from the rain-style shower head come in contact with my skin.

Ryder, being the gentleman that he is, pulls my front to him, stepping out of the spray so that I can fully be under it. I close my eyes and tip my head back, grateful for the hot water and the scent of Jimmy's soap, opposed to antiseptic.

He smooths the hair back from my face again, rinsing off the scent of jail and infirmary before reaching behind me where my shampoo and conditioner sit on the shelf. I hear the bottle open before his hands are back on me. Lathering the suds, his fingertips massaging my scalp are heaven. I relish in the gentle but firm touch.

Rinse and repeat with the conditioner. I still haven't opened my eyes, I don't need to. Or maybe I'm afraid that if I do I'll break. I'm dead on my feet and I promised myself a good shower before I would let that happen. I take a deep breath as his hands start massaging soap onto my skin. "Coconut," he says.

I then open my eyes, taking in the deepest blacks that regard me with nothing but adoration. I lean forward and whisper, my lips across his, "thank you."

He has no idea how much I'm thanking him for. It's so much and yet I feel like *thank you* is not enough. He kisses me back, once on my lips, and another to my forehead before he continues with his hands, massaging soap onto my back, my sides, gently over my ribs and around my front. It's not sexual, it's thorough and considerate. When he nears my thighs, I pull back. The small shock is evident on his face as I shake my head.

"I need to shave."

Whatever look was in his eyes is gone as he nods his head. "Was worried beautiful, I thought maybe you didn't want me to touch you after what happened." He swallows the rest of his words, looking at me for an answer.

I shake my head slightly, "nothing like that handsome. Just wanna shave."

He hands me my purple razor from the shelf and I waste no time, nor do I try to be modest. As Ryder lathers his own hair, I shave from my armpits to my ankles. Ryder does his best to be discreet but I can't help but feel his eyes on me. I know he's watching, and I'm sure if I turn around I'll see evidence of him doing so. I set the razor back on the shelf and move under the spray to rinse off. I wasn't wrong, and Ryder's arousal is plain on display. Never being a shy one, he does nothing to hide it. I'm not offended.

Bending down in front of me, his hands smooth up my legs, washing the suds off. His strong hands move up around my hips, across my lower abdomen and down between my thighs. Never paying enough attention in any one place, simply providing the service of cleansing me thoroughly.

I look down at him crouched in front of me, this beautiful, strong man who has never harmed me in any way. The man with gentle hands and black eyes. The man I sang to in jail from the deepest part of my soul. A man I swore who I would tell I loved if I got out of there. A man currently in front of me doing his damndest not to take me as his in the most intimate way possible, but at the same time claiming me more than if he'd done so.

"Make love to me, Ryder."

His eyes snap up and his hands remain hooked behind my knees. The silver in his eyes shine bright around the black and his hidden pupils dilate. Slowly standing, his hands keep contact with my skin. They move above my knees, over the back of my thighs, past my rear and up my back until they're joined behind my neck.

I watch the water droplets fall off his black hair and down his face, falling once they reach his chiseled jaw. His voice is gruff, full of emotion. "In bed," is all he manages to reply before he shuts the water off. I'm meticulously dried, as he half-hazard throws a towel around his waist and walks me across the hall to the spare room in Jimmy's apartment.

The door is shut after we enter and Ryder makes a half-assed attempt to dry himself before leading me to the bed. The covers are still pulled back, which isn't like him. He always makes the bed in the morning. I noticed that when he came to me in Indianapolis. Ryder's life is structured and a made bed is part of that structure.

I don't think any more of it as he leads me to the side and guides me to sit down. Removing the towel from my shoulders, he leans forward until I'm forced to lay down.

"Head up to the pillows, beautiful."

I move into the normal resting position, head on the pillow and legs bent in front of me. Ryder follows and rests between my spread legs, first kissing my belly button, then my chest, neck, jaw and mouth. His forehead rests gently against mine as he speaks against my lips.

"I want you so fucking bad beautiful, I do. I'm trying to take my time here, but Christ I missed you so much."

I hear the agony in his voice, wondering how it must have felt for him. Not knowing if I was okay after the guard beat me. He would have gotten word that I was alive, and in the infirmary I'm sure, but mentally, who knows. He wouldn't have. I didn't even know.

I reach up and run my hands along his back, over his shoulders and into his thick hair.

"I'm here, and I'm okay Ryder."

He pulls back to look me in the eye, once again with nothing but sincerity and love reflecting from them.

I can't help but ask again. "Make love to me Ryder, please."

My breath hitches a little on the please, because I'm not used to asking for anything. I am used to doing everything on my own and I hope he realizes exactly how important this moment is—for me to ask for something.

His fingers sift into my hair, and his thumb traces around the edge of my stitches. His eyes follow the path and I watch the crease between his brows form before he settles his eyes back on mine.

"Anything you want beautiful, I'll give it to you. That being said I'm not giving this just because you asked, I'm giving it because I want nothing more than to make love to you, and I want to be the only one who does it, forever Elle."

I close my eyes as the first tear of emotion escapes and runs down my cheek. Ryder catches it with his lips before it has a chance to hit the pillow. "I love you Elle. So much it fucking kills me sometimes."

Warm lips touch my own but it's brief. "Open your eyes, beautiful."

I do as he says, staring at the handsome man above me. The way his dark hair falls over his forehead, the way his eyes light up when he's looking back at me—leaves me breathless.

"I love you. Just you, *all* of you. I told you to keep me babe, but I'm also keeping *you*. It's been hell not knowing what was happening with you these past few days. Complete fucking hell. Now that I have you back, I'm not lettin' you go beautiful. Not ever."

This time it's me who crashes my lips to his. He holds my face, ever the dominant one, taking over the kiss. His tongue dances with mine, he tastes better than I remember. I keep my hands in his hair, holding on so tight and afraid to let go.

One of his hands lets go of my face and runs along my side, over my hip and between my legs. His mouth detaches from my own and moves to my neck. Licking, sucking and kissing his way down. He feathers wet kisses along my collarbone, paying extra attention to the bruising there from where the guard held me down.

More tears escape, I can't stop them. It's futile to try. "Shhh, beautiful. Don't cry."

Of course it makes me cry more, until he latches onto my nipple and his hand settles into the wetness between my legs.

"Christ, always soaked for me. I love that about you beautiful, I just fucking love you." His thumb circles my clit while he puts two fingers inside. I pull on his hair and he lets go of my nipple in favor of my mouth. I gasp against his lips when he touches me in exactly the right spot. I'm so close. Only he can take me there that quickly.

I reach between us, grabbing hold of his well-endowed self, guiding him toward my entrance. Removing his fingers from inside me, he brings them up between us, putting them in his mouth to clean them before entwining his hand with my own.

I guide him inside, and allow him to claim my other hand as he pushes in. "Don't close your eyes beautiful, you know I hate when you close your eyes."

So I keep mine locked on his.

Green on black.

I allow him to see into the deepest part of me, the part no one sees. The part that needs a moment like this in order to see it. I let it all go, out through my still-watery eyes and into his clear, sharp ones.

Wrapping my legs around his back, Ryder pushes deeper, harder, but still in that slow punishing pace that will no doubt leave me breathless.

"Greenest eyes I've ever seen, stay with me babe."

I'm glad he knows this is hard for me. Not the sex part, the part where I let him in. It's not the toughest thing I've ever done, but it feels like in this moment, I am giving myself to him.

"I'm with you, handsome."

I lean my head up and claim his mouth with my own, falling back to share the same air. Out through his mouth, into mine and back again. I feel the perspiration on his skin, and I tighten my legs, lifting my hips up to meet him thrust for thrust.

I know he's close, I am too. I look deep into his eyes when he rotates his hips against mine, shattering me into a million pieces, making it nearly impossible to keep my eyes on his. Strong hands grab the side of my face and he kisses me with such fierce passion as he lets go on a growl.

I let it go again too, and I let him take it.

All of me—scars included.

Chapter Seven

I feel the soft brush of fingertips as they travel across my back, up over my shoulder blades and back down again. His other hand is on my hip, thumb making slow, lazy circles on my naked skin. I sigh in contentment, having had the most wonderful sleep. Opening my eyes, I see Ryder's sated ones watching me. I decide to go for honesty because it's been proven that life can change too quickly, and tomorrow, as much as I hate the thought, I might not wake up next to him.

So I tell him, "I missed waking up with you."

The side of his mouth tips up in a smile, before he softly touches his lips to mine. "Missed waking up with you too beautiful."

I hum against his mouth in appreciation. "How long have you been awake?" I ask.

"Never went to sleep."

The tenderness in his eyes melts some of that ice around my heart. Or dare I say all of it? Here, in this moment, I don't feel cold. I don't feel the hate and fury that threatens my existence. I just feel him, and me.

Together.

I know once I leave the sanctuary of this bedroom, the ice will start to come back. It's my invisible armor against the outside world that has dealt me a shit hand. But right now, I focus solely on the man in front of me and how he makes me feel. The fact that he makes me feel at all is something I will forever cherish.

THE UGLY ROSES

Glancing over at the clock, I see it's almost eight in the evening. I could easily go back to sleep but the rumbling of my stomach says otherwise.

Ryder smiles softly. "Ready for dinner, beautiful?"

I smile a little and nod. A few kisses are rained on my face before he helps me from bed. I stretch the aches out of my body, and Ryder unabashedly takes in all of me.

"If we were at home I'd tell you to stay like that and join me at the table. But I heard someone in the kitchen not too long ago and I'd rather not share your body with anyone else."

I wrap my hands around his waist and settle my head on his chest. I kiss him above his heart and speak to his taught skin. "Thank you, Ry, those words aren't big enough, they never will be. But thank you."

He kisses the top of my head and holds me close while speaking into my hair. "No need to thank me. Just be with me, that's all the thanks I need."

I lean my head back and get up on my toes to kiss this incredible man. I wish I was better with my words. Saying I love you is big, but it's not big enough. It's not enough or exactly what I want to say to him.

I settle on the kiss and get dressed. When I find the right words, or the right way, I'll show him.

* * *

I sit on a barstool beside Ryder at the island in Jimmy's kitchen. There are three extra-large pizzas from Vinnie's on the countertop. Denny, Ivan and Jimmy had already devoured one and a half before I finished my first slice.

53

"Laura called, Jay. I told her you were good but give her a ring so she doesn't show up here in the middle of the night." I nod at Jimmy. She'll lose sleep not completely knowing what happened to me in jail and not being able to talk to me now that I'm home. "I will."

I take a swig of my beer, watching Denny in my peripheral vision. He hasn't said much since I got back, but he keeps staring at the stitches on my forehead and the bruising around my eye. They all gave me a gentle and warm welcome when Ryder and I finally left the bedroom. Aside from that, it's been pretty quiet. Especially Denny. Not being one to beat around the bush, I cut my eyes to his when I find him staring again. "I'm alright Denny."

If I wasn't already facing him I would have missed the pain that crossed his face. I have no idea where it came from or why it's there, but it's gone as quick as it came. He scrubs his hands over his face, nodding his head at the same time Ryder puts a firm hand on my thigh, squeezing a little.

I'm not an idiot so I take Denny's deflection and Ryder's silent warning to let it go.

"Good to have you back, darlin'," he says before leaving the room and going downstairs, giving me a shoulder squeeze on the way. I wash down another bite of pizza with my beer and look to Ryder, "Not my story to tell, beautiful."

I nod. "I respect you for saying that."
He kisses my temple in thanks and I see Jimmy shaking his head at me, not in disappointment seeing as he has a smirk on his face.

"What's with the smirk, James Rourke?"

Using his full name gets his attention. He tosses his leftover crust toward Norma, who's curled up on the couch and comes over to put his arm around my neck, kissing the top of my head. "Love you Jay, and happy to see you letting some of that love come back to ya. You deserve it."

I fight the tingle in my throat as he says this quietly into my hair. Ivan, who hasn't put his phone down misses the conversation, or perhaps he misses nothing and is just looking busy on his phone.

Ryder takes my hand and holds it to his thigh, lacing our fingers together when Jimmy lets go. I lost one warmth but gained another. I allow this thought to settle deep in my bones as I finish what's left of my dinner.

Only when my belly is full and my eyes begin to fall does Ryder take me back to bed.

Chapter Eight

Ryder

I peel the clothes off her perfect body. Scars and all—she's perfect. She's mine and I appreciate her every inch as I unravel her like a Christmas present. Before Elle, I never enjoyed taking my time with a woman. It was a means to an end. As much as I like the female form, sometimes I wouldn't even bother getting them all the way undressed. Call me a selfish prick but once I got what I needed, I was gone. I'm not a complete asshole, I made sure they got what they needed too; but I can't remember the last time I wanted to wake up next to someone.

There were a few before Anna, my only long-term relationship, if you could call it that. But since Elle I never truly knew what it meant to want to actually *be* with someone, aside from fucking them that is.

I lay her down on the bed, and worship her like I always will. She deserves to be worshipped. She deserves my mouth on every part of her body from the tip of her toes to the top of her pretty little stubborn head. As much as I miss her sass, which she will surely get back, I'm enjoying my time with her the way she is right now. I love all parts and sides of her; I'm not picky when it comes to Elle.

I love her.

I pay special attention to all the places that make the soft mewl sound come from her throat. I pay more attention to the ones that make her pull my hair.

When my mouth is covered in her scent, I finally lay my lips on hers. She has no problem kissing me after I've gone down on her and it makes me love her that much more. So that's what I do for the next hour, love her until she's moaning my name and can no longer keep her eyes open.

Only then do I fall beside her, pulling her naked and sated body over my own before I fall asleep for the first time in three days.

* * *

I feel the warmth of her mouth moving across my chest. She mumbles something I can't quite catch, and I open my eyes taking in her riot of dark brown hair, the loose curls falling over her shoulders and across my arm. She's the most beautiful fucking woman I have ever met and I'm the lucky bastard who gets to wake up with her mouth over his heart.

"Mornin', handsome."

Her sleepy, raspy morning voice travels straight to my dick, but I push that aside in favor of studying the softness of her eyes in the morning. She frowns in her sleep, and I always rub the pad of my thumb softly between her eyebrows and run my hands through her hair. She doesn't know I do it, but even when she used to fall asleep on her couch, before we ever slept together, I smoothed out those lines of worry.

"Mornin', beautiful."

Her eyes always change when I call her beautiful, not in a soft way but in a way like she doesn't believe me. It's lessened over time but it's still there. I choose not to bring it up right now in favor of putting my lips to hers.

She settles down on my chest, head resting on her hands. I touch the area around her stiches, once again moving her hair out of her face. I like to see all of her—nothing in the way. "I hate that he marked you Elle, it fucking kills me that I couldn't protect you."

She sighs, "There's nothing you could have done, Ryder."

"If it's too hard, I get it. I'll understand. But I need to know what happened. It's killing me not knowing anything other than what I saw on that video, and what the report said. I want your version, Elle."

She closes her eyes for a minute and I almost think she's not going to tell me. Then she opens them and surprises me as she relays everything, from the time the guard first teased her with a tray of food, to the time she left him unconscious on the floor. My hands form into fists for the majority of the conversation, and as if she could hear my earlier thoughts she reaches out to smooth the frown on my face. I soften completely at her touch like the pussy I am for this woman, and kiss the palm of her hand.

I hold it against my face, and she brushes her thumb over my bottom lip before pressing her mouth to mine. She hasn't told me she loves me, she never said it back when I said it to her. But she doesn't have to.

I can feel it.

"I want to take you home beautiful, I wish this shit was over with so I could take you home."

Her eyes soften at my words; I know she wants to go. This place isn't her home anymore. As much as she ran to the cottage—and let's be honest, she was running—she ran *toward* her home, not away from it. I see the love that she has for her friends, but this is not her place anymore. She doesn't relax like she does at home. Her eyes don't light up here when she watches Norm chase a squirrel like they do when she watches her run toward the water.

Perhaps when this is over she'll spend more time here, but I'll do everything in my power to keep her with me.

"I want it over too. Still no news from Cabe or Maverick?" I shake my head, disappointed in myself for not being able to find this fuck. "I have a name, I have a picture. I just have no paper trail to lead me to him. I've hunted people before. This is not a first for me, Elle. The last two I hunted were in the jungle and before that it was Iraq. My team were successful on both missions and I feel like a fucking failure seeing as I haven't turned over any new stones in the past few days."

Elle rests her head back on my chest, staring toward the window.

"You've tried Ryder, that's more than I can ask you for. If you have other work to get back to I understand. But I can't leave. Not just because of the judge's orders, but because I won't sleep until I know where he is. I'll never truly feel safe."

I flip her over on her back, she's shocked for a moment until I get my face close to hers, pinning her body to the bed.

"I don't quit, and whatever else I had lined up can wait. You may not have understood it but let me clarify for you, when I said I loved you, I mean *I fucking love you*. That means wherever you go, I go too. And when your life is in danger I won't stop trying to protect you until the fucker is either dead or behind bars. That's part of what me loving you means. I'm not going anywhere, beautiful. I told you to keep me, which also means you're stuck. You understand?"

I don't miss the shine of unshed tears in her eyes. Where my stubborn bitch went I have no idea, she'll come back soon. For now, I settle with the understanding on her face before I taste her lips, and then the rest of her.

* * *

Elle

I look over the rim of my rocks glass to one of my best friends. Laura's hair is a mess, typical because she has most likely spent the majority of her week worrying about me and her kids, opposed to looking after herself. Laura is a worrier, and I hate that I caused her anymore stress, but if the roles were reversed, I would be where she is right now; deathly afraid for my best friend and wondering when all of mess will come to a head.

"I want my friend back, I want you to see the kids. They miss you," she says.

I think about my friend's children with a heavy heart. I miss her kids, those I took on as my god babies, and I miss my own child in heaven. I sacrificed for them because it was for their own safety, but even knowing that it doesn't make it any easier.

"Me too Laur, you know I do, but I need some more time."

She sighs, "You won't stop until you find him and that's what I'm afraid of. What if he isn't after you anymore, Jay? And what if all of this is for nothing, well not *nothing*, I know you need to sleep at night and get justice for your family. I just worry about how long it will take, and hope it doesn't steal you away from what you have now."

I look at my best friend, the only girlfriend I have. She could be right, I know I have some good in my life right now and I am thankful for that. But she's right when she said I won't sleep.

"I won't live looking over my shoulder, Laura. That's not living. Besides, it's not just about me and my family, it's about a psychopath being out there and he could do the same to someone else that was done to me. It's not just about justice.

It's about stopping this from happening to anyone else. I mean, if I quit—if Ryder and his team quit looking and something like what happened to me happens to someone else—well, I wouldn't be able to live with that."

She nods in understanding. "I get it Jay, and I do. I'm just not happy about it. You're finally back, albeit partially."

I take another swig of my wine, swallowing the bittersweet drink to avoid eye contact.

"Fuck, I get it," she says, shaking her head while her eyes absorb every one of my features. She sets her cup down on the island top in Jimmy's kitchen. "You're not staying, are you? Even when this is over, you're not staying."

Sadly, I shake my head, "I don't think I can Laura, not because I don't want to. I'd love for this place to feel like my home again… but it doesn't. I didn't come back here and feel any peace or comfort. I felt *nothing*. It's like my time here is over, it served its purpose and now it's time to move on. The only fraction of pleasure I felt at coming back here was because I would get to see you and Jimmy. Aside from that, there's just nothing."

The words were but a whisper on my lips near the end. She's the first person I have said that out loud to, but if I had to guess Ryder already knows because he's so damn perceptive. I watch as tears form in the corner of her eyes. Laura doesn't have a lot of female friends. Neither do I because we've always had each other.

"I knew this was going to happen. Wait, that's a lie. I didn't know until I saw you when you came back. I always thought that once it was over, things would somewhat go back to normal. But when I watched you leaving the courthouse with Ryder yesterday it was like *I knew* that this was going to happen. I want to tell you that I'm happy for you, because you more than anybody deserve some happiness, but it's not any easier for me to deal with. Please don't think I'm selfish for thinking that, but fuck—I missed you, hooker."

The tears bubble over and I wrap my arm around her, keeping the other on my drink, pretending I don't see Jimmy, Ryder, Brad, Ivan and Denny's eyes on us from the other side of the room. I hold my friend until the tears have dried on her cheeks before topping up her vodka and cranberry cocktail.

"I'm not trying to make anything harder on anyone Laura. I miss you guys too, more than you know. The only thing we can look forward to is when this is over we can talk on the phone again, and make plans to see each other. I could lie and say it will be hard to leave here, but it's not, Laura. That scares me as much as it makes me happy to finally say goodbye to it all."

She nudges my shoulder. "It's because you have someone incredible on the other side of that. You're saying goodbye to the old life and hello to a new one. I'd happily say hello to a man like Ryder, too."

Giving a small smile to my friend is my only answer. After everything that's happened I hope that the worst of my troubles are behind us. The Beckers, Braumers, and Claudias will hopefully take a back seat in our lives so we can move forward. To where I do not know. But away from the heartbreak and drama, and hopefully toward something much brighter.

"You ready, love?" Brad says from behind us. Wrapping his hand around the back of Laura's neck and kissing her on top of her head. She closes her eyes at the contact much like she does every time he touches her. I envy what they have, the closeness—nothing between them.

"No, but I need some sleep." She leans my way, giving me a one-armed hug. "Call me if you need anything. Or just call me for nothing, I don't care."

"Will do babe," I say, hugging her back and adding an extra squeeze for good measure.

I'm not the same woman I once was and I know that's hard for her. Losing someone who you knew better than the back of your hand isn't easy, especially when they come back as someone else, not just inside but on the outside as well.

I watch them go and Denny moves to take the seat next to me at the island. The other men are sprawled between the sofa and the kitchen table that never gets used.

"How you holding up?" he asks.

I feel like I should be the one asking him that question but I don't, I sense whatever his worry was before and whatever underlying pain he has is not something he wants to talk about.

I know all too well how that feels so I don't push. "I'm alright, Denny. I'm tired, but I'm alright."

He nods. "I wish shit here was going faster for you Elle, I do. But we haven't one fucking clue what to do next. We're at a dead end here, and until something else pops up, or Shawn shows his face, we've got nothing else to go on. I wish we had better news for you, but we don't."

"Not your fault, Den. I'm grateful for the help even if we haven't got quick results."

Ryder comes over from the sofa in the living room, and soon the other two follow. "Alright, Cabe called. He's been digging into finding the missing computer that was never registered in the evidence log. He hasn't found it but he thinks he found Andrew Robert's online storage account."

"So? What does that mean? Did he find anything that helps us?" I ask.

Ryder shakes his head. "I don't know if it helps us yet. There's a lot in there to go over. He found one file titled 'J' and it held the same photos of you that were in the basement. He said everything is encrypted, password protected, whatever the fuck that all means. All I know is that he's working on getting us more information."

I rub my temples, grateful for the non-useful info but incredibly tired and done with this week. I've done well today. I've shown my face, been pleasant enough around people and stayed awake for almost the full day. What I really want to do is crawl into bed and not come out until all this is over.

Not bothering to say goodnight, because I've always been a fan of a good Irish exit, I leave the kitchen and head to the bedroom.

Chapter Nine

Not too long after I climb under the covers, Ryder joins me. I roll to my side so I can face him and rest my body on his. He's so much bigger than I am and I can't help but feel comforted by his size.

"Where's your family, Ryder?"

I settle further into his chest, running my hand through the mild scattering of chest hair. He never talks about them, and I'm not sure if that's because he doesn't want to or because of what happened to mine. Maybe he just doesn't want to share? Maybe he doesn't want to upset me?

"Only child, beautiful. My Dad died when I was eleven. Mom didn't fare too well but she never let me down as a parent. I swear to this day I never saw anyone so heartbroken over a loss. My parents loved each other, weren't afraid to show it either."

His lips settle into my hair and he continues. "Mom did everything for Dad. He also did everything for her. She lasted eight years after he passed, before she went too. Cancer."

I press my lips to his chest, directly above his heart. "I won't say I'm sorry handsome because 'I'm sorry' to me is an admission of guilt and I hate those words. I have nothing to be *guilty* for, but I do feel badly that you didn't get more time with your family."

His answer is a squeeze of his arms around my body, followed by his lips on my forehead. "Respect that, beautiful. My dad died of a stroke, days after he had it. Mom had months when she found out before the cancer took her. I got to say goodbye, and for that I'm grateful. You didn't, Elle. So I'm the one who feels badly for you, everyone deserves a goodbye."

I turn my face toward his torso, breathing him in. There's no better smell in the world for me at the moment. My favorite smell is Ryder.

"Handsome?"

Fingers run down my spine, settling on my waist with a squeeze. "Ya, beautiful?"

"I can't have children." I clear my throat and clarify. "I don't want children. I don't want to hurt again. I don't want to experience anymore loss, I just can't handle it."

Strong hands reach under my arms, hauling me up his body until I have no choice but to brace my arms on either side of his head.

Those beautiful blacks explore my face, searching for what I don't know. If he's searching for a lie then I know he won't find it. I can't have children.

I don't want children.

I did.

I don't anymore.

I was not made to be a mother aside from parenting the love of my life, my Lilly. And now that she's gone I can't picture myself with another child. Not because I don't want to necessarily, but because it hurts too fucking bad.

I've hurt enough. Haven't I?

It's been almost five years since I was pregnant. I don't know if I could go through that again. Cory was a wonderful father. He was there for me when I needed him. But he wasn't there to fall asleep with me at night. He wasn't there for the very first kick. He wasn't there the first time I stuck my head in the toilet, not because I didn't want him to be, and not because he didn't either. But because we didn't live together.

Cory had his home, and I had mine. We lived our separate lives but included each other when we needed to. I won't say that I did it all on my own, because I didn't. But lying in bed at night, having pickle cravings or back aches, and wanting someone to feed and hold me, well that's when I felt alone.

Of course I never said anything. I was always good at hiding how I felt. I have also always been good at doing everything on my own.

Jayne O'Connor

Harley Green

Elle Davidson

No matter the name, I'm still inhabiting the same body. The body of a woman who never asks for help. I once went two days without hot water because I refused to ask for it. Laura bitched my ear off that the landlord was useless, but after those two days of searching online, researching what kind of boiler we had and what I could do to fix it, I did.

I fucking fixed it.

By myself.

I hate asking for help, and doing so recently has made a huge dent in my armor. It's not a bad dent, per se, but it's a dent none the less. I focus on the handsome man below me, wondering, worrying that perhaps his life includes more life than mine does.

If he wants children, I am certain that I will not be able to give them to him. I've been down that road. I've been there, done that. Got the fucking t-shirt heartache and misery to go along with it.

Got the grave too.

I can't go there again.

Had my tubes tied to prevent it.

"I'm not going to lie and say I've never wanted kids Elle, because I have."

I sink further into his warmth, placing another kiss above his heart.

"Handsome, please don't let me keep you from having a family." I no sooner get the words out before I am rolled to the side, my head resting on his arm with his hand in my hair, his other arm on my hip. He has my undivided attention.

"Beautiful, I pictured kids when I was eighteen. Did it again when I was overseas, watchin' guys get pictures of sonograms from their wives. It hurt Elle, watching grown men cry over someone they never met.

"I never got it, not at first. Not until I watched a buddy of mine, he was from Canada too actually, skype with his woman giving birth in a hospital. Never watched her, because that was his. But I watched him, you couldn't not."
Ryder shakes his head, lost for a moment. "Never saw so much love. Watching a grown man fall apart, missing the birth of his boy. It cracked me, beautiful. It cracked and broke me really fuckin' hard."

I feel for him, and the man that missed the birth of his child while fighting to keep the rest of us safe. Because it's not just the Americans keeping the Americans safe, or the Canadians keeping the Canadians safe. Canadian, American, nationality is important but the goal is the same. In my mind, *we're one.*

THE UGLY ROSES

We always have been.

We're just *people.*

We're human beings with the same goal.

Keep each other safe, at any cost.

Sometimes that cost means missing the birth of your child. And god bless the fucking people who gave that up in order to keep the rest of us safe in our homes at night. Ryder has been one of those people, and my heart aches not to provide him with a safe haven for his offspring.

"I can't give you what you deserve, Ryder. I can't." I end when my breath hitches, pressing my lips back above his heart.

"Shhh, beautiful," he says into my hair. "You're not getting me."

Calloused hands pull my face from his chest. Only when he knows he has eye contact does he continue.

"I broke that day beautiful. I won't lie because I did. Watching him hear the first cries of his kid, and not being able to be there for it was devastating. But know I'm honest when I tell you I will take your beautiful face, lovely body and your stubborn head, with or without children."

A sob I can't stop escapes but he presses on. "I love you Elle, more than I ever loved anything. If you come without kids, I'll live with it and be happy to do so. You're mine, beautiful, and I wasn't fucking joking when I told you I'd take you any way I could have you. Children are a bonus, but I don't need them to love you any more than I already do."

Blubbering into his chest I reply, "I know what having a child feels like, Ryder. You deserve that and so much more, you deserve everything. I can't be here and know that I took that away from you no matter what you say. You saw what that man went through; you should have the same opportunity Ryder. And the only one taking away that opportunity is me. Just me, Ryder."

I pull my head out of his chest and look into his glassy-black eyes. "You deserve it all, Ryder. You're a good man. Too good. Don't let me stop you from creating little men such as yourself because I promise you, the world would be better, so much more whole *with* them than *without*. Don't deprive yourself and the world of that, Ryder. Because this world needs a lot more people like yourself. Don't let them or yourself down."

I'm rolled over, Ryder's heavy body crushing my own. I don't complain, I never have and I never will. I accept his weight when his hands frame my face. "I'm letting myself down if I let you go, Elle. If I let myself down, then everybody else goes with it. There's no debate for me, there's no second guessing. It's just you. The answer is you, beautiful. I don't need anyone else, I don't need kids. Because I just want you. Only you, babe. You're mine, you're keeping me and I'm keeping you. It's as simple as that." Warm lips touch mine before he continues. "Nothing else, beautiful. No one else, just Ryder and Elle."

He grinds his hips into my own as his tongue seeks purchase in my mouth. He swallows the sob that escapes my lips.

"But you'll resent me. One day Ryder, you'll hate me for depriving you of something you could have had. I can't live with that and you shouldn't either."

Strong lips silence mine. "It's done Elle. The only thing I *don't* want to live without is you. I already told you you're stuck with me, so you're mine. Mine forever beautiful, and I promise you so long as I have you I don't need anything else. Nothing. Just you, all of you."

THE UGLY ROSES

He touches his lips to mine. "Scars included."

Chapter Ten

It's been five days

Five days of nothing. Five days with little news about anything or anyone. I want to pull my hair out. I want answers and I have none. It's driving me insane. We've all more or less been staying at Jimmy's. Denny, Ivan and sometimes Maverick apparently have rooms at The Rockport, a nicer motel about a mile up the road. One of them always seems to end up on the couch regardless.

Some nights they say it's because they've had too much to drink, but I know it's so that Ryder is not the sole person watching out for me. I don't think the guys mind it much, Ivan added to his tattoo collection, courtesy of Jimmy, and Maverick spent one night down here so he could get out of the bush while Denny took over up north.

The guys have been busy down in the shop for a while. Ryder said they had some business to go over before they went down there and I didn't bother to follow them because I assumed it had to do with something else they were working on. Jimmy is sleeping off his three-night working bender where he either drank with his new buddies or painted until the wee hours of the morning.

So it's just me, stewing up here and waiting for *something* to happen. I look out the window to the street below and notice Andrei Patrov exit Jimmy's shop and get into a sleek, black car. Footsteps coming up the stairs notify me of Ryder's arrival and I turn to watch as he stalks toward me. Dressed in dark jeans and a long sleeve black Henley, his beard still unshaven and his hair all mussed give him that just fucked look that I can't get enough of.

He knows it too.

When he reaches me he cups me around my nape and puts his forehead to mine. "Gotta go out for a bit beautiful, Denny's downstairs beating on the punching bag. I'm guessing he'll be down there a while until he works through his shit. I'll be back in a few hours. You need anything or you need to go anywhere just ask him."

I shake my head. "I need to get out of here, Ryder. I'm going insane and it's not like me to be a sitting duck, stuck in one place for so long."

Kissing my lips he says, "I know beautiful. Cabe sent through some files he was able to get from Andrew's online storage. He also sent some shit he found on him from university; I left it on the table downstairs. Take a look, it doesn't make sense to any of us but it might make sense to you."

Grateful that I finally have somewhere to direct my energy toward, I nod. "Good, it'll give me something to do other than just sit here."

I shake out of his embrace but he pulls me back by my arm. "I love you Elle, and I hate to say it but I would rather have your ass stuck up here bored out of your mind, opposed to out there and dead. It's tough, I get it. I sat in the same spot in the desert for days on end. Trust me babe, that sucks a lot more than being in a cushy apartment. We'll get him, I promise you that."

I know he's right but it doesn't make it any easier. Nor does it help my temper in any way. "I know Ry, go do what you need to do."

With one last kiss to my lips, only deeper and involving tongue, he leaves.

A few moments later, after the fog has cleared I trudge down the steps into the shop. The workout room is off the back hall and I hear Denny pounding away on the punching bag. I don't bother him but head to the table, seeing part of my life spread across it.

I see everything from my case file to photos, and one new folder sitting on top of it all. I open it up, noticing some transcripts of Andrew's from university. He was computer tech student who made good grades while he was there. Some of the notes in the folder were written in a .docx file Andrew made. They mean nothing to me.

A few spreadsheets are included regarding *ANIG Tech Solutions*. Someone has circled profit margins showing a considerable amount of money withdrawn, but it makes no sense because as far as Cabe or Revenue Canada is concerned the company never made that much. Not on paper anyway, just in Andrew's files.

I skim through the rest of the small folder. There are a few noise complaints from the university that were filed against him and I'm assuming his then girlfriend, Sarah Hillbrand, who by the looks of what I'm seeing trashed his apartment and got charged for assault for throwing a lamp at his head.

Other than that, it's useless information.

I pace around the table, wondering if his awful behavior started back then. Surely it didn't happen overnight? If this bitch threw a lamp at his head he must have deserved it. But it makes no sense that she was charged and not him.

Who the fuck knows.

I need to get out of here, I need to walk and I need a drink. I can't think in this place anymore, there's no clarity. It's like everything here is stagnant after five days of nothing. Walking back upstairs, I put my armor on, trendy hat included. All the images from my past run through my head as I walk back down the stairs, back to the beginning.

THE UGLY ROSES

***

I sit idling behind the parking lot at Frank's in Jimmy's Chevy truck. I want to go in and have a drink, but I can't yet. I purposely drove on the main street out front so I could avoid this, but being the stubborn woman that I am I couldn't stop myself from turning around back to see where it all went down.

I haven't been back to Frank's since the night I was taken from this very parking lot. It's changed and I have no doubt that was Frank's doing. There used to be only one light on the back of the building, and one lamp post at the side of the lot. Now there are four brand new lamp posts that light the lot up like daylight.

There are also two security cameras on the back of the building that has new lights along it as well. I remember that evening vividly, like it was yesterday. It was much darker, but having walked the same way home for years, the little light was enough to get me onto the back street and on the sidewalk to home. I never feared that walk, nor did I need the light to guide me there.

Now I've turned into a woman who fears the dark. Not because of the dark itself, but because of what could be hiding in the shadows beyond my line of sight.

I stare at my surroundings and allow the nightmare from my past to unfold in front of me; the van up ahead, the feel of Andrew's hand on my mouth with the soaked cloth, and the reflection in the van window of two men looking oddly alike. I now know that's because there were two of them—twins.

I see the man in the wrinkled suit, keys in hand as he watches me get taken against my will but makes no move to help me.

I see it all.

I killed Andrew, and I have no remorse for doing so.

I can't kill his brother, because I can't find him.

I let the anger bubble up, pushing out the weakness I felt in that moment and allow the frustration to set in. There's only one person available at the moment who I can let it out on, and for the first time in five days, I have a destination.

Chapter Eleven

The mailbox tells me most of what I need to know.

R. Wallace.

It's the same name from the police files I had memorized and I waste no time in surveilling the property.

It's shit to say the least. The shrubs haven't been trimmed and lawn needs to be cut. The paint is peeling off the front door and the windows could use a good scrub. It's not a complete shithole, and I'm certain his previous home was better kept than this one. I take pleasure in knowing this is most likely due to the divorce that ensued a year ago, and it looks good on him. Detective Miller told me Wallace never reported my abduction because he was at the bar to meet up with his side piece and he didn't want his wife to find out. Divorce looks good on him, serves him right.

Karma can be a nasty bitch, and I'm about to show him just how awful that can be.

I look just like anyone else out for a late-night jog, aside from the fact that it's almost pitch dark, and I'm wearing tall black boots and not running shoes. I've been waiting near the park, scoping this place out and I'm finally going to make my move.

I jog lightly up the sidewalk and when I'm sure that nobody is paying attention (not that I've seen anyone give two shits about what happens in this neighborhood) I bolt up the lawn and edge along the side of the house.

There's no garage so I know he's not here. I also locate the back entrance and peer in the filthy windows along the way. No lights are on aside from the light above the oven in the kitchen.

Perfect.

When I get to the back door I take a look at the hardware. There's a deadbolt which I wasn't prepared for so instead of messing around with it I check the two windows that are on the backside. The one that seems to be the bathroom window doesn't open. I walk eight feet to my left and see the kitchen window is open, just a crack.

I reach up and push the screen. It slides on the track, enabling me to push the kitchen window open all the way. It's about five feet off the ground, and thanks to all my hard work with Brock and Denny, I have no trouble using my arms to pull me up, placing my foot on the ledge and pushing myself in.

I brace my hand on the edge of the sink and try not to knock over the dirty dishes in the sink. I can tell they've been here a while because what food isn't completely hardened on them fucking stinks.

I bring my other leg in through the window and while squatting on the counter I pull the screen closed and shut the window tight. I don't want anyone hearing what's about to happen here.

Time to get the lay of the land.

The kitchen is small. It has a round wooden table with four ugly wooden chairs, chairs with spindles on the back. They're outdated, but sturdy. Most likely a hand-me-down that survived years of abuse but still lasts because it wasn't poorly crafted like everything else made in the last twenty years, purchased at a big box store.

There's an opening in the middle of the kitchen which leads to the living room. It too is ugly with its brown carpet that looks like it's been here for forty years. It holds an easy chair, a worn plaid couch and small television on the opposite wall.

THE UGLY ROSES

There's a picture window at the front but the heavy curtains are pulled closed. The main door has a small rectangular window but it's the ancient kind where the glass looks wavy so I know I won't be noticed.

I head down the hallway to my right and locate a washroom on the right side, a small utility room after that and a bedroom on the left. That's all that's in this tiny little house.

Nothing fancy here either. A double bed with sheets askew. It smells like nothing in here has been washed in a while either. There are nightstands on either side of the bed with a closet to the right, and a dresser at the end.

I go to the closet first and note the multitude of cheap suits that are in there. Apparently, the man still has his job. There are a few shoe boxes and some extra bedding. Nothing out of place, no weapons to be found.

I open up the drawer in the nightstand, thankful for the leather gloves I have on. There's a multitude of porn magazines, and an opened tube of lubrication. I guess he was in too much of a hurry to close it because it's leaked all over the drawer. I lift out the magazines and find a few condoms, but other than that, no bibles or weapons in here.

I do the same to the other side table and dresser drawers, finding clothes and some mail and other useless shit.

One thing that catches my eye before I leave the bedroom is the only picture on his dresser. It's of him and what I assume is his ex-wife, if the rings and white dress are anything to go by. He doesn't look too bad in the photo, and he looks happy as well. His sandy-brown hair is well kept. He's not handsome but he's not really ugly either. I'm guessing he's maybe in his forties now, and in the photo he looks to be maybe in his late twenties. Either way, he was clean cut and not at all who you would expect to live in a dump like this place.

Forgetting everything in here because I don't need to remember it, I head back to the kitchen to gather what I need to be ready.

I wonder if he'll remember me when he gets home.

Probably not.

He may have forgot about me by now, the scared woman from Frank's parking lot who he refused to help, all because he was afraid his wife would find out that he was there to meet another woman.

He'll soon know what it feels like to be scared and helpless.

I'll make sure of it.

***

It's almost ten when I see the lights flash through the small gap between the curtains. I don't budge from my spot at the kitchen table. My ass is numb from sitting still for so long—and so is the rest of me. I'm not sure why I do this to myself, embrace the numb again. But with Ryder out on business and me alone, I don't feel so guilty for reverting to my cold-hearted self. I need a little of her back right now.

Just for a little while.

I hear the car door slam and the jingle of keys as he makes his way to the front door. I hear the twist of the lock before he enters, wisely locking the door behind him.

Too bad he doesn't know the danger lurking outside is already sitting at his kitchen table.

THE UGLY ROSES

A curse follows the flick of the switch. The light doesn't come on because I loosened the bulb. The less light coming from the living room, the better.

I listen to his footsteps as he nears the kitchen. I hear a thunk on the way and assume it was him dropping his briefcase on the table in the entryway.

His back is to me as he enters the kitchen, heading for the light switch that I know illuminates the kitchen beside the rear door. He succeeds, and my eyes take a moment to adjust after sitting in the dark for so long. It's not enough to set me off guard.

Robert Wallace turns around and lets out a surprised huff of breath before his keys drop to the floor. He's seen me, but I don't see any recognition in those eyes. "Who are you? What are you doing in my house?"

I allow a small smirk on my face, the most my lips have tipped up since I was taken to jail. I'm not worried about him running away—I'm faster. So I take a moment to survey his appearance.

Much the same as before he's wearing a cheap suit. His hair is not as well kept as it once was and he looks as though he's gained ten or twenty pounds. Judging by the amount of beer and takeout containers in his fridge I'm certain I know where it came from.

You see, meeting up with a side piece of ass at a bar while your wife is at home will do that to a man. Meaning he no longer has a nice home cooked meal and a good woman to iron his suits. No. Now he's on his own, lacking the ability to properly care for himself.

I clear my throat and respond, "I'm offended Robert, you don't remember me?"

He swallows, clearly caught off guard. I can't imagine he gets much ass anymore but he's not hideous. Therefor I think for a moment he may have thought I was one of his conquests after or during the time he was married. It seems as though as quick as that thought runs through his head it leaves him.

"No, I can't say that I do."

I have to hand it to him, he's polite. He's also incredibly dull. I located his pay stubs while in his bedroom. Therefor I know he works nine to five as an accountant for Westin & Young.

Boring.

He also looks mildly afraid which pleases me because I don't plan to soothe that in any way.

At all.

I take a pull of my beer sitting on the table, completely at ease and not at all concerned. This day was coming, I knew it and now he will too.

"In total I think I spent around twenty-two thousand dollars that month."

He's confused, which he should be. To my delight, he asks. "For what exactly?"

My smug grin returns as I remove my feet from their propped position on the table. "For surgery to fix my face and housing after my attack a year ago."

I watch the recognition coming across his face before he slowly steps backward toward the door. I waste no time standing upright, moving at a speed Brock would be proud of as I dodge the table and swing my right leg out, connecting my foot to the back of his leg.

As expected, he goes down on one knee. I grab a handful of his suit, swinging his upper half backward as I quickly jab the outside of my hand into where his neck meets his shoulder. He curls right, and I take the opportunity to grab his left arm and rear it up behind him, forcing him to stay on his knees and double forward.

"What do you want? I'll call the cops!"

This only makes me happier seeing as he and I both know there isn't a fucking thing he can do right now. He's weak, he's gained weight, and I can smell the gin on his breath from his after-work cocktails from whatever waterhole he frequents now. He'd be stupid if he ever set foot into Frank's again, and I know if Frank knew who he was he wouldn't let him in there regardless.

I twist harder and force him to his feet, guiding him toward the kitchen chair. Once I have his ass planted there I pull the zip tie out that I found in his utility room and secure his hands behind his back. He fights me, but a quick flash of the knife I don't plan to use makes him stay still.

"You know Robert, I've thought about this for a long time. What I was going to do with a man such as yourself. More specifically, one without any fucking balls."

He lets out a grunt. I slap him on the backside of the head then move to the other side of the table; resuming my position with my feet on the table and beer in my hand.

I can see his distaste when I light up a cigarette. I know he doesn't smoke because I didn't find so much as a lighter in the house. I also never found an ashtray so I use the kitchen table. It's ugly anyway, what's a burn mark or two?

Character, that's what I call it.

My comment clearly offends him, not that I give a shit but it's nice to get a reaction out of people when you plan to beat the fuck out of them.

"There was nothing I could do!" he spits out. "He was bigger than I was and you were already in the van! I couldn't help."

His comment strikes the fire smoldering in my veins. After I was taken may be a bit foggy, thanks to the soaked cloth that covered my mouth, but prior to that my memory is pretty fucking vivid.

I slam my beer bottle down on the table, smashing it.

"Liar!"
I drop the bottle and swing my right arm out, connecting my fist to his cheek, loving the crack that follows.

His head snaps back and I follow with my left, catching him off guard. I might have been able to punch with my right before, but my left was weak. Seeing the amount of blood coming out of his mouth, it's not anymore.

"Tell the truth!"

He spits, drool and blood running down the front of his shirt. I don't at all feel sorry for him.

I feel nothing.

"I c-c-couldn't help."

I wipe my hand across the table, sending the newspaper and salt and pepper shakers flying before slamming my gloved fists on the table.

"Like fuck you couldn't have. You could have made a scene. You could have called for help. You. Did. Nothing."

I hit him again, square on; breaking his nose.

"You were twenty feet away. You *could have* jumped on his back. You *could have* used the keys in your hand to gouge his fucking eyes out. You *could have* called the fucking cops after I was shoved against my will inside the van!"

I round the table, fed up with the obstacle. He starts singing like a fucking canary.

"Alright! Alright!" His words come out jumbled. I think I broke a tooth. Once again, not that I care. "I didn't want my wife to know where I was! She couldn't know!"

This sorry excuse of a man is anything but a man, that is. "A good man doesn't cheat on his wife. A good man goes home to her after he's done work. A good man would not have watched an innocent fucking woman being kidnapped. A good man would not have waited two fucking days before he went to the cops."

I get down in front of him, my face inches from his. My voice low, determined. "You, are not a good man. You're not a man at all."

The blood is pumping through my veins, the visions of what happened to me running rampant in my head. The nightmares are fighting to get out, fighting to have some purpose after the fucked-up mess that has been the past year. They flow from my mind, down through my arms and out through my fists. One nightmare at a time.

What's left is bloody, slightly broken, but still breathing when I cut the zip tie off his hands. I grab the neck of my broken beer bottle along with my cigarette butt off the table and exit the back door.

I don't lock it behind me. I don't look back.

Chapter Twelve

I walk through the front door, completing a quick scan of the patrons, recognizing a few but not bothering to say hello. There's an old friend of my dad's in the corner, where he always used to sit. One of the town sluts that Jimmy used to fuck, and maybe he still does, sits along the far wall. I'm only here to see one person and that's Frank. He stands behind the bar in his usual garb of jeans and a worn out plaid shirt. I notice his short hair is now completely grey and briefly wonder if life has been hard to him.

I walk to my once familiar barstool toward the end of the bar where I can see the rest of the place with my back to the small stage. He's rinsing a few beer mugs in the sink and asks, "what can I get ya?" as he turns around.

The mug that's in his hands nearly drops to the floor, but the old man catches it in time. "Sweet Jesus, woman," he says while his eyes roam my face, "you look good Jayne, different but good. About time you came back to see me, I've missed you girl." He smiles, "Missed your smart mouth too."

He's rambling, and I give him a little smile. I made sure to check myself in the mirror of the truck to make sure there was no blood on me after I ditched my sweater and gloves. I still have my hat on because I needed the privacy.

"Good to see you too, Frank."

His smile falters. My voice is not the same as it used to be, along with my face and dark hair I'm sure it's a lot for him to take in.

"Double Vodka and Perrier with lime, please?"

Like the good man he is, he wastes no time in making my drink. He also knows I prefer the liquor on his top shelf so he pours the Grey Goose and takes a shot for himself. Clearly, he wasn't prepared for my visit.

After setting my drink down in front of me I take over. "How's business Frank?" He sees right through my bullshit and like the straight shooter he is he calls me on it. "Don't you bloody well think you're gettin' off that easy. You're lucky the wife ain't here or she'd be all over you like that cheap perfume Prissy wears."

I can't help but let out a small laugh. Prissy is Priscilla, the tramp in this very bar tonight who Jimmy used to fuck (maybe still does), and who wears so much perfume Frank once told her if she wanted to keep drinking here she had to tone it down because he didn't like sneezing while mixing people drinks. It wasn't sanitary.

"Can I finish some of my drink first?" I ask him, not quite ready for questions, just wanting to enjoy my five minutes of freedom. I also respect the man enough to not just get up and walk out the minute I want to close myself off.

"Half of it," he barks, shaking his head. "Things are the same around here as they've always been. People come, people go…some of 'em stay."

Frank's easy, and I love that about him. Every answer is simple and there's no need to argue over anything else or make it complicated.
"Heard you were back." He tells me, "Your partner in crime was down here a few nights ago after work and didn't leave 'til Brad pulled her ass off her stool at eleven."

I shake my head at him. "Tequila in her hand and Moody Blues on the jukebox?"

Tossing back a swig of Guinness he says, "Tequila nights never finished in that woman's eyes until she sings *Nights in white satin* at the top of 'er lungs. She still can't carry a tune for shit."

I chuckle at my old friend, thankful in the moment for useless banter like old times before he pulls me out of memory lane. "What's goin' on with ya girl? I know ya better than ya think. You ain't back here 'cause ya missed home. *Longing* ain't the expression on your face right now."

I'd be shocked, but Frank is bartender. Has been for decades. He's over sixty and has run this place since I was a baby. He's had all that time to read people and study them from the other side of the bar top.

He's damn good at it too.

It also helps that he's known me since I was a kid because my father was one of his regulars who stopped by for a cold beer after work. I don't waste time beating around the bush or giving him the long story because he doesn't need it. "There were two people involved in my attack. One is dead. The other needs to be found."

"Shittin' Christ," he curses. "I knew somethin' wasn't right. Laura blubbered in here one night after you left about you being scared and takin' off. Never asked her more and she never supplied but I guessed."

Sad, light blue eyes meet mine and he continues. "Never in all my life did I feel like a failure for not havin' a good security system around here Jayne, never in my life. You know we don't get much trouble being on the outskirts of the city, never thought I needed it."

I shake my head at him. "It's not your fault that there's fucked up people in this world Frank, you can't change that and neither can I." After taking a swig of my drink I reach out and put my hand on his. "It's great what you've done out back, it is Frank. But even those cameras wouldn't guarantee that you'd get a license plate number or a clear picture of the man taking someone. It was out of all our hands."

Angrily wiping his hands on his towel, he says, "that prick out there in the parking lot shoulda' helped ya. I never found out about it 'til two days later. Detective came in here and gave me his name, asked me how much he had to drink. Then he told me he'd seen you being taken, breaks my fuckin' heart girl that he didn't help you. Breaks my heart."

Not liking where the conversation is going, but also knowing Frank would probably buy the entire bar a round of drinks if he knew what I did to the man we're speaking of, I move the conversation along. "I met someone," I say, not hiding the small smile on my face. Frank takes this news well.

"I'm happy for ya girl, I am. He happen to be the one walking into the bar with his eyes lasered on your back?"

I turn my head and watch my Viking of a protector stalking toward me. He must have changed and showered before he noticed I was missing because he doesn't look like the sweaty mess he should after beating a bag.

"Nope, that's just a friend," I say as Denny reaches me, sliding onto the stool beside me.

"MGD if you got it, please," he says.

Frank reaches blindly into the beer fridge, knowing it better than he knows the back of his hand. He doesn't take his eyes off us as he un-caps the beer and places it in front of Denny. Giving me a nod he heads to the other end of the bar to refill a beer and Denny faces me after he pounds back half of his own.

"You should've told me you were leaving. I don't like being skipped out on, Elle. That was a shit move and you know Ryder's going to have both our asses when he gets back. You put me in a tough fucking position."

Slightly ashamed but not remorseful, I nod my head. "Sorry, it had to be done. I needed out of there."

Downing the rest of his beer in two big gulps he says, "Next time you're going to go all Mata fuckin' Hari again let someone know. I wasn't even out of the shower when Cabe called to tell me your cell signal was coming up on the other side of town. I was two steps away from barging into Wallace's house to stop you, Elle. Two steps!"

I nearly choke on my Vodka. "Fuck Denny!"

"Don't *'fuck Denny'* me! You could have been hurt, Elle. What if you got there and he wasn't the useless fuck you remember? What if he spent the last year doing what you did? Training to fight, to protect himself. You didn't know what you were walking into, you do something like that you figure him out first. You don't ambush someone you know nothing about in his fuckin' kitchen and hope to shit you make it out alive."

Feeling slightly embarrassed, because he's right, I ask myself *what if* Robert Wallace was a bigger man now? Not the pussy I met in the parking lot? Who knows what would've happened. I don't think about it and I don't dwell on it any longer because I'd rather not talk about it.

"It's done," I say, knowing nothing can be changed and nothing can be taken back.

"Damn right it's done. Ivan's been sitting outside watching you while I cleaned up a mess I didn't want to clean up, Elle."

"What the hell is that supposed to mean?"

He leans close, speaking low. "It means, that not only did I make sure he wouldn't talk, I gave the prick a phone to call an ambulance. I knew you didn't want to kill him, if you did, he'd be dead. But he needed a little help after your fists got ahold of him."

Nodding my head in thanks, I push my glass toward Frank's side of the bar and he picks up the signal to come and refill it. "Frank, this is my friend Denny. Denny, Frank."

Frank gives his hand a shake. "Nice to meet ya. Stay away from Prissy." I look in the mirror behind the bar and see the hookers hawk eyes zeroed in on my friend. Denny looks confused so I say, "she's on par with that waitress from the pub you took me too Jacksonville." Recognition hits but he semi-ignores me to dive into the second beer Frank set in front of him.

"Which one of ya caused trouble?" Frank asks, but immediately looks to me. I don't know what he's talking about until Ryder and Ivan slide up to the bar. Ryder takes a seat beside me, and Ivan takes the one next to him.

Ryder's eyes are furious as he spins me around on the stool, prepared for a tongue lashing I'm sure. Frank's eyes dance over us all until they settle behind me. "Wasn't talking about those two Jayne."

He clears his throat.

"Detective, what can I do for you tonight?"

Fuck.

Chapter Thirteen

"Just need to talk to Jayne and the security crew here," Detective Miller says.

Frank's confused, but Ryder sticks his hand out. "Good to meet you Frank, I'm Ryder." They shake, and Frank asks, "Security? You lookin' after my girl here?"

Ryder responds quickly, "Doing my best, sir."

Deciding to keep the conversation pleasant, I toss in. "Ryder owns a company called Callaghan Security, Frank. He's the one I was telling you about earlier." Seeming pleased with where this is going and who I ended up with, Frank smiles. "Well let's get everyone a drink then, can't have any friend of Jayne's goin' thirsty. What about you, Miller? Off the clock yet?"

Detective Miller shakes his head. "Not yet Frank, just need a word," he says, nodding toward me.

"What can I do for you, Miller?"

Rubbing his hands over his face he looks at the men beside me. "You want an audience?"

I shrug. "I don't hide anything from them. What's this about?"

Hands on his hips he says, "I just got a call that the home of *Derek Stratus* was burned to the ground." Clearly, he can see the confusion on my face so he adds, "The guard who attacked you in prison."

Shaking my head, I look him in the eye. "Can't say Im hurt by that news but I'm not sure why you're telling me?"

Frustrated, he goes on. "Derek was *inside* the house when it burned down. Fire chief says the propane had to have been leaking for it to go up like that. Now, it could be a coincidence, but I don't really believe in those."

I go to open my mouth, but he holds up a hand. "To top it off, while I was at the hospital investigating a gang murder, I got called back over to trauma where a man was brought in half beaten to death. Wouldn't have recognized him, but the name sure put up a few red flags for me after I heard about the burning house. Robert Wallace, same man who was out there the night you were taken," he says while pointing toward the back lot.

"She's been here for hours, catchin' up with me. Wasn't her," says Frank.

I silently thank him. I know I have only been here for just under one hour, but he knows or assumes I'm guilty because otherwise he wouldn't have bothered to put his two cents in.

"Callaghan, I know we had a deal and I hope you didn't step beyond that," Miller says, and I have no idea what deal he's talking about.

"My team and I were with our lawyer, Andrei Patrov, putting together a case against Derek Stratus for the assault and attempted rape against my woman. You can call him if you'd like to confirm."

Miller looks to the floor and shakes his head. "Look fellas, I'm not saying some people don't deserve what they get, but I still have a job to do."

Ryder nods in agreement. "I respect that, Detective. But I won't lie and tell you that I'll lose sleep at night knowing the spineless prick who couldn't defend an innocent woman is in the hospital, and the scumbag piece of shit security guard is cookin' in house as we speak. In fact, I think we'll all sleep a little lighter knowing this world has one less sick fuck in it. Appreciate what you do Miller, and I told you we'd help in any way we could with the case. But this is not part of that and don't expect me to lend a hand in figuring out how either of those incidents happened tonight."

Resigned with the knowledge he'll have no help and knowing that there's nothing more to get from us, a defeated looking Miller says his goodbyes. I feel bad, a little. Only because he does have a job to do and I don't like lying to him because he is a good person. But for the most part, Miller likes to stay on this side of the law. I give him forgiving eyes. He gives me sad ones and a small chin lift before he walks out of the bar.

"Anything you care to share with me, beautiful?" The warm, whiskey voice washes over me, his breath hot on my neck. "Not here, handsome."

He pulls back a fraction and takes a swig of the beer Frank lined up in front of them. I look to my old friend and silently thank him again. He raises his Guinness in a toast, and I follow suit, downing what's left of my vodka, pushing it toward him for another.

***

Eight shots of Vodka in and I signal for another. Jimmy has joined us. Laura and Brad came in after, and for the first time in five days I feel lighter. It's probably the Vodka, and it might also be the aggression I got out earlier, but either way it's nice to be out and surrounded by men who are protecting me so I can let loose, even if just a little.

"It's nice to see you out, Jayne," says Brad, giving me a one-armed hug and kiss on my temple. "You too, Brad. Thanks for coming last week by the way. I appreciate it." He gives me a no-nonsense look, because there is no other place he would have been besides having my back at the courthouse.

I give him a hug and notice Laura weaving her way back from the bathroom laughing. She's stayed off the Tequila so far, which is a blessing. She halts mid-giggle when the woman behind her speaks.

"Who are your friends, Laura? You'll have to introduce me." Prissy's face comes into view and she pauses scanning all the men at the bar. Well, Ivan, Denny and Ryder since she knows the rest of the crew.

I wait to see who she locks eyes on. She hasn't noticed me yet, and I'm not sure if she'll recognize me. We never spoke much simply because I don't often speak to people who I don't respect. Last I heard, Prissy had three kids from three different fathers, one of them used to go to the same daycare Lilly did. I felt sorry for the kid because he was behind due to the fact Prissy never took the time to teach him anything, thus adding to the shit list of things I don't like about her.

I gotta hand it to her though, she's still kept her body in shape at the ripe age of thirty-two. She's not hard on the eyes with her long reddish-brown hair and heart shaped face. But it's what's underneath all that shine that takes away from it. Prissy was, and always will be the bitch who treats everyone as if they are less than her. Regardless of the fact she has three baby daddies, the men still flock to her.

Slowly sauntering toward the bar, she leans between Denny and Ryder. I left my stool to talk to Brad and it looks like she'd gladly take that place. "Mind if I sit here while I wait for Frank?" she asks Denny with sultry eyes and wet lips. He shakes his head, unaffected by her charm and already warned by Frank before she came over here.

"It's taken," Ryder simply says, going back to nursing his beer.

"Well you guys aren't much fun tonight, are you? Who's got you in a mood, maybe I can cheer you up? Buy you a drink, my treat?" She places her hand on Ryder's Henley covered arm. I note this one is white, not the black one he wore when he left Jimmy's.

"Go back and work your corner Prissy, this is still our end of the bar," Laura says. She and I have always been picky with who we hang out with, we like good people and honest ones. This has also been our end of the bar since we were old enough to see over it, and later, drink at it. Frank doesn't chat with people like her. He gets a barmaid to serve their drinks while he sidles up next to a good and honest regular, like Laura or myself.

She mock laughs, still trying to impress my hot as hell security crew. "Oh, Laura I just wanted to meet your friends."

I cut her off. "They're not here to make friends Prissy, they're here for my homecoming."

Her face sours. "It's *Priscilla*, and you are?"

I smirk, "Same sweet bitch I was when I left here. Only now I'm back due to my involvement in a pending murder investigation, being questioned about a man being burned to death, oh, and I just got out of jail for assault charges, so don't piss me off today."
Her face blanches at the news. I watch it fall. "Jayne?"

"The one and only. I suggest you head on back to your corner and remove your hand if you plan to keep it. Word on the street is that I *kill* people," I say with mock horror.

Her hand drops like it's on fire, completely caught off guard. Stuttering for a moment, she straightens her spine and hitches her purse up higher on her shoulder. "You always did know how to make a grand entrance, didn't you Jayne?"

I answer her, "so long as you've got the exit part covered, we're good."

Huffing out a breath she retreats to her corner of Frank's.

"Sure, did miss you around here girl," Frank says with a smile on his face. He always gets a kick out of Laura and me. We mean no harm, and it provides him with entertainment.

"Jay just doesn't like rotten pussy encroaching on her territory, Frank," says Jimmy.

"If I'm not mistaken, it wasn't too many months ago you went *home* with that rotten pussy," Frank deadpans, causing the whole group to howl in laughter. Jimmy holds his hands up, "Hey, I made it as far as the front door and no further. I haven't touched that in two years. Honest."

He's upset Frank would think so little of him, but Jimmy has only a few standards; tight ass, round tits, hair long enough to pull and good teeth. Jimmy believes if you don't take care of your teeth, you probably don't take care of what's underneath your clothes.

"Alright, who wants tequila?" Laura shouts, and Jimmy and I exchange a look. I've had fun, I feel good. But it's time for me to call it a night. Ryder catches my pleading look and hooks me around the waist. "Ready to go, beautiful?" I nod in answer and start to say my goodbyes, but not before Laura shoves one tequila for *old times* down my throat.

Chapter Fourteen

"You tipsy, beautiful?"

Rubbing my face against his bare chest, I confirm. Not off my rocker, but definitely feeling good. Ryder tugs my shirt over my head and continues with the rest of my clothing until I weave before him in nothing but my birthday suit.

"Did you have a good night?" he asks against my neck, placing kisses along my shoulder, working his way up. I sigh, "I did."

Putting his hands under my ass, he lifts me up and I wrap my legs around him. Crawling on his knees he moves us forward until we're in the middle of the bed before he lays me back down. Continuing his assault with his mouth, he unwraps my legs from around his waist and moves his tongue south. Mid tongue swirl in my belly button he asks, "What were you thinkin' tonight Elle, going to that house?" He continues his assault, making it hard to answer questions.

"I was thinking, I-ugh…" I stop mid-sentence when his tongue makes one long lick up my center. He stops completely. "Answer me."

I fist the sheets. "I was frustrated, fed up, pissed off and sick of sitting around! Aggghhh, thank you." His tongue swirls around my clit, pinching it between his teeth. "Why Elle?"

Frustrated, I grab his hair. "Because I did!" I try to bring him forward, but he likes his hair pulled. He just sits there, staring at me, his lips an inch from where I want him most. Big black eyes stare back at me, and he places one quick kiss before he removes them. "Why?"

At wits end I let go of his hair and throw my hands up before leaning on my elbows to see him better, "Because I had to! Because I need to *feel* something! Because I needed to let it out! I went to Frank's and stared at the fucking parking lot, thinking if I can't catch the other brother, I'll start from the beginning which was that useless fucking accountant who wouldn't help me! That's why! Happy?"

Obviously not because he stares at me from between my legs like I should have given him more. So, I do. "It felt good Ryder. It felt fucking good to beat the shit out of someone, to not feel weak. Maybe if he had helped or called the police, I wouldn't have been tortured for three days." I take a breath, "So that's it, I don't feel bad about it and I'd do it again. If you can't live with the kind of person, I am then get your mouth away from my pussy so I can make myself come. Take it or leave it because I don't see myself changing any day soon."

No sooner do the words fly from my mouth when my body flies through the air. Too fast his right arm went under my back, sending me up, over and back down, face first in the mattress. I push my knees and elbows into the bed to sit up and tell him exactly what I think when his hand collides with my ass.

"Fuck!" I shudder, caught off guard from being on the verge of what would have been an incredible orgasm to being slapped on my ass. Ryder's weight settles on top of me. My knees are still to the bed while he sooths the spot he smacked me with a gentle hand. "That was a stupid fucking move Elle, incredibly fucking stupid. You put Denny in an awkward position, and you could have gotten yourself killed! Denny told me what he said to you. He was right. What if Robert Wallace wasn't so fucking helpless anymore? You had no idea because you didn't plan it out."

Being held by his weight on the bed, I turn my head to the side and glare at him, our faces a foot apart. "It's done, I can't change it. I don't regret it."

Pulling up, his heavy hand lands on my other ass cheek. "You son of a bitch!" I shriek, not at all impressed and ashamed because as mad as I should be, I'm dripping down my leg.

"You didn't think. That's what gets you killed, Elle," he rasps in my ear.

"Oh, and you *thought*? What the hell was that all about with Miller? Huh? Don't think I didn't notice your clothes were different when you came into the bar. While I was out kicking ass, you were having a bonfire; a very big one by the sounds of it!"

Leaning down, he licks up my spine to the base of my neck. I can't stop the shiver running through my body. He notices. "You're mine. I told you I look after what's mine. I've been pretty fucking patient with you, Elle. I gave you space, and we've gotten to where we are now which is me telling you that my patience has run dry and I'm done fucking around. Bottom line here is nobody touches you but me, and I know you like when I touch you," he says while licking and kissing his way back down, over the swell of my ass and back again.

"Why would you do that for me? I'm grateful he's dead, but why Ryder? What if you get caught?" I feel his head shaking against my back before he moves his head back beside mine. "I won't."

I sigh. "You're not invisible, Ryder. Nobody is."
Moving the hair out of my face, he kisses my temple and moves to my earlobe. "We are, we were, and we won't get caught."

I huff in annoyance, not at all impressed with his answer because I hate the thought of anything happening to him, especially because of me. It's incredibly noble of him, and Ivan I'm assuming, along with Patrov. But we could have taken up some form of religion instead and prayed that Derek

Stratus died of a flesh-eating bacterium he could have contracted after my teeth sunk into him.

Instead, he put his life on the line.

For me.

"Ryder, thank you but it's still not any different from what I did tonight, you-ooof!"

The air whooshes out of my lungs when his hand comes down on my ass again.

"Quit talking about it, Elle. I'm tired and pissed enough as it is. Drop it."

"Dammit Ryder, I'm not trying to—*fuck*!" Two more slaps come down and his hands dive between my legs. "You're soaked so don't deny me. As much as I love reddening your pretty ass, I'd rather fuck you to sleep. I love you, Elle. I do. But we're not talking about this anymore tonight. I'm hard and I'm tired. So, can you be quiet for five minutes so I can take care of that? It's been a long night."

Being tipsy, and unable to help my smart mouth, I can't stop the words before they come out. "Just five?"

The answer is Ryder's hard shaft in one long drive deep inside me. "Gah, fuck!" My back arches like a cat and he grabs a hold of my shoulder with one hand. The other slides down between us.

"I love fucking you, Elle. I love making love to you too, but I thoroughly enjoy fucking you." Gathering my wetness with his thumb, he moves it up to my rear, circling the tight muscle while keeping pace with his thrusts.

"You with me, beautiful?" he rasps. I shake my head. "I'm with you, handsome." In one smooth motion, he pushes in at the same time he trusts. It's exquisite and full, causing my entire body to shiver.

"God you feel good," he says, pulling his thumb out and replacing it with his finger. Pulling back on my shoulder, he helps me up onto my knees and wraps his arm around my body, his hand tight on my chest. Warm lips work their way up my neck, and I reach up, holding onto the back of his hair.

"You're almost there," he says as he sinks his teeth into my shoulder. It wasn't a question, he knows my body better than I do. Reaching down I put pressure on my clit with the heel of my hand and reach my fingers out to cup his balls. Adding the right amount of pressure that I know he loves.

"Fuck!" he growls, picking up the pace. "I love you!" My legs start to shake at the emotion in his voice and the orgasm coming out of nowhere. Like a fucking train, he rams into me, and his finger drives deep into my rear, while pinching my nipple between fingers on his free hand.

"God!" I wail, shuddering in his arms. Violent tremors take over every part of my body and make me thankful he doesn't let go.

"No, just Ryder," he smartly says in my ear, squeezing his arms around me as he too shudders against my back.

Removing his finger, he puts an arm to the bed and lowers us down to the mattress. That's the last thing I remember before falling asleep with Ryder still inside me.

Chapter Fifteen

I watch Norm in the back lot. Sniffing around, doing her business and snapping at some sort of insect that keeps buzzing around her head. Ryder is to my right, doing something on his iPad and drinking his coffee. He's been quiet this morning, but I brush it off and chalk it up to a busy night.

Denny doesn't seem to sit still for too long. He's ten feet away, tinkering with some truck part at the picnic table with Ivan. Jimmy, being the last one to show his face comes out the back door while I'm on java number two.

I'm mid sip of the hot brew when Jimmy plops down into the chair beside me. "How's your ass this morning, Jay?"

The hot liquid sprays out of my mouth all over the white plastic table and Ivan howls with laughter, sweet deep laughter while Denny chuckles lightly. Ryder just shakes his head beside me.

"Sorry man forget where we are sometimes," Ryder says, not at all fazed by the comment as he continues to tap away on his screen.

"No apologies needed," he says toward Ryder and turns his head to me. "You needed an ass whooping after yesterday, Jay. I love you, but that was even too ballsy for you."

Wiping the coffee from my mouth I glare at my friend. "First, you know not to try talking to me before I've had two cups of coffee. And second, what the hell? We've all made some shitty choices in life. I'm lucky enough mine didn't backfire and neither has the rest of what you guys got up to last night. End of discussion."

Jimmy is obviously in the loop about what Ryder and his team got up to because he doesn't ask questions. There's a buzz at the gate and Ivan goes to check it out, allowing Andrei to enter.

He's still dressed smartly, but today he lacks a coat and is only wearing a dress shirt, unbuttoned at the top with sleeves rolled up. I'm surprised to see he has ink there but he always did seem pretty badass, so it just adds to his flair for me. His dress slacks and crazy expensive shoes complete the Patrov wardrobe today.

"Morning gentleman, and lady. How's everyone this morning?" Denny gives a grunt and a nod, Ivan smiles big, replying, "perfect day, suns shining!"

Jimmy and I nod, and Ryder shakes Patrov's hand.

Standing on the other side of the table blocking my view of Norma I look up to him. He has a smile on his face and his Russian accent graces my ears. "Go on any adventures lately, my fearless one?"

I smirk and shake my head, "nothing too exciting. Have any bonfires lately my favorite Russian one?"

Trying to hold back the smirk but failing miserably he replies, "No, just a barbecue. Unfortunately, the meat was foul."

I throw my head back and laugh, a full-bodied kill myself laugh. "Oh my god!" I say through the tears at the corner of my eyes. Everyone else is in the same state as I am. Doubled over with laughter, howling at the hilarity of a man who is normally so serious.

"Fuck that was good," cries Jimmy as he wipes the moisture from his face with his t-shirt.

"Coffee, Patrov?" Mine is nearly empty and still sprayed across the table.

"No thank you, I'm only staying a moment," he says.

Grabbing my empty cup, I get up from the table on a wince, ready for more java and in need of a bathroom break after the first two.

"Are you alright?" Andrei asks, concern written all over his face. He probably thinks I got hurt last night. I did not, and unfortunately Jimmy feels the need to share. "She's fine; Ryder just decided to give her ass his handprint for taking off last night."

I don't bother turning around to see the expression on Andrei's face. I keep walking, coffee cup in hand, to the kitchen.

Men.

***

"Jimmy's heading to the grocery store. He wanted me to ask if you needed anything, but I think it was his way of hinting at you cooking us dinner."

I smile from my spot on the couch with Norm. That's definitely Jimmy. "Yes, I'll make him a list."

Ryder comes around the coffee table and sits on it, facing me. "Need to ask you something, Elle." Not liking where this is going but prepared to be honest, I answer, "Anything."

He nods his head and looks down at the floor for a moment. Running his fingers through his hair, he brings them back between us and rests his elbows on his knees. "You don't have to tell me, but I'd like to know because it's been bothering me." His eyes finally meet mine. "Is there, or was there something going on between you and Detective Miller?"

I'm taken aback, mostly because I didn't think anyone would ever pick up on that. I should have known better when it came to Ryder because he's too smart. Loving the honesty, we have I answer him, nodding slowly. "About a few months after my family were killed, yes I was with him."

Closing his eyes for a moment, he exhales. "How long were you with him?" I shake my head at his assumption. "It wasn't like that, Ryder. We had spent some time together, but I was only with him for one night. In the way that you're thinking anyway."

"He cares for you," he says.

"I know he does, but not like I care for you and you care for me," I tell him. Reaching out and grabbing my hands, he pulls them to his mouth. Kissing the palms on both of them he says, "It was hard at home. By home I mean North Carolina. I see the way men look at you, but I knew at that time you had no interest in pursuing anything. Now, you've changed. You're still you, but you've opened up more. You're coming back out from those walls you built around you and now it's harder to see other men admiring you. Especially ones you know, and ones you've been with.

"I need to know how serious it was Elle, because the way that man looks at you makes me want to do things that would probably fuck up my reputation as a decent human being and a leading security expert. I can't *not* know because now that you're coming out from behind these walls it makes me wonder if I'm not the only one who was waiting for them to come down so they could barge in and claim you as their own."

I'm completely baffled by Ryder's words and his insecurity. Perhaps I haven't given him enough to make him understand that I'm not going anywhere? I don't know, and I'm confused.

"Ryder, Miller was a long time ago. He slowly became a friend after my parents died and one night, I was at a bar. Not Frank's, a different one, having a few drinks. I didn't want to be around my regular people, I just wanted to be invisible. Anyway, long story short he was there and after a few glasses of wine I went home with him. It was a shitty move on my part, I was depressed and lonely. I took advantage of our friendship by seeking something to make me feel good again."

Ryder holds up his hand. "Beautiful, it's not taking advantage when he looks at you like he does. He *wanted* it."

I shake my head at him. "That's my point Ryder, I knew *he* did. I *didn't*. I just wanted to be held for a night and to forget. He provided that and he was kind, he still is kind. Regardless, it was wrong of me when I knew I wouldn't want more. I apologized the next morning, he wouldn't accept, so we've been acquaintances ever since. He dropped a few hints here and there afterwards, but I knew I wasn't ready, and I didn't want to be rude, but I knew when I was ready it wouldn't be with him."

Placing another kiss on my wrist he replies, "It's not easy knowing you've been with him. Not gonna lie, beautiful I don't like it."

I agree with him. "I get it, Ryder. I met Tina, then Anna, then I had the pleasure of hearing about Claudia, trust me, I get it."

He shakes his head, "But it doesn't feel the same because I have no respect for any of them Elle. You respect Brian Miller and that's what makes it harder. I'm not good with this shit, neither of us are. But I think we're doing well right now and

I'm trying really fucking hard to explain it to you from my point of view without making you upset or me getting pissed off."

I look into his eyes. "That's part of what last night was, wasn't it? You weren't just pissed because I went to Robert Wallace's house. You were pissed with the way Miller looked at me when he was leaving, weren't you?"

I pull my hands from his and sit back on the couch, watching him scrub his hands over his face before he looks at me. "Not gonna lie to you Elle, that's why I'm sitting here. Yes, it pissed me off. On top of you going to Wallace's house, it pissed me off. I'm not saying I took it out on you because I thought you would act on it, but, well, I was pissed."

"You were more than fucking pissed Ryder, I can barely sit on a hard surface let alone a soft one."

He shakes his head at me. "You were dripping down your legs woman. Don't try and tell me you didn't like it."

I throw my hands up, but still speak rather calmly. "That's not the point, Ryder! The point is that instead of asking me about it you allowed it to fuel your already burning frustration toward me for leaving. I'm not saying I didn't enjoy myself, but the motivation behind your actions was because of another man, not because I went against what you asked me to do. Essentially, to me that says there's an underlying issue of you not trusting me, because if you did, if you *really* did Ryder, you wouldn't have batted an eye at Miller's actions. You would have let it slide off your shoulder because you knew without a doubt, I'm *yours*."

Standing, he paces around the coffee table. "I didn't bring this up to fight with you Elle, I didn't. I don't want to. I trust you, I do."

I stand up. "You don't, not if you took it out on me like that you don't. Actions speak louder than words, Ryder. You know that as well as I do." I walk past him to the steps leading to the shop.

"Where are you going?" he shouts behind me.

"With Jimmy to the grocery store," I say, walking down the steps.

"Ivan!" Ryder shouts again, "you're on tail duty at the store."

Ryder doesn't bother following me down the steps. My eyes meet Jimmy's and he knows I'm in a mood. Wisely, because he knows me so well, he says nothing as we head to the truck. Ivan steers us left toward the SUV he drives, I say nothing as we all get in and head to the store.

Chapter Sixteen

"What'd he do now?" Jimmy asks as he tosses random shit in the cart.

"He asked about Miller, and I told him. Then I figured out that's what he was stewing on last night when he painted my ass red." Jimmy chuckles at my rendition of the night before.

"We all know Miller wanted you but even I know he's not your type. Want me to talk to Callaghan?"

I shake my head. "Don't stir the pot. I doubt he would listen right now anyway. Let him be stubborn for a while."

"You know all about stubborn, I won't argue with you. But if this shit's still brewing at dinner, I'm saying something. I love you Jay, and I'm not letting you fuck this one up."

I stop the cart and face him. "You're shitting me, right? I'm the only one who can fuck up a relationship?"

He smacks my already sore ass and Ivan chuckles from the end of the isle when I wince. "Don't put words in my mouth Jay, I hate when you do that. You know damn well what I'm saying."

"Fuck," Jimmy says under his breath. A woman about my height with black hair is headed our way.

"Jimmy!" she cries, not at all noticing me beside him, or pretending not to.

"Randi," Jimmy says casually. I snicker knowing exactly who she is. I pretend to ignore him, and act extremely interested in the canned kidney beans beside me. Who knew there were so many different types of beans?

"I tried calling you, like *twice* the other day. And last night; I tried last night too but it went to voicemail," she whines.

God, why are women so dense?

I know Jimmy is very upfront with the women he sleeps with. He's not a bad guy, at all. He's just not ready to settle down, regardless of the fact he's over thirty. He tells them straight 'don't expect anything more from me', and yet they still come back for more.

"Look Randi, I'm not trying to be an asshole, but I told you straight up what I was about. I apologize if you heard me wrong, but I think you're just not listening. I'm not interested in a relationship with anyone. I'm a busy man and I got a lot going on at the moment," he says, very diplomatically I might add.

"Yeah, I see you're busy," she huffs. "Couldn't even get you to stay for coffee and now you're already out with someone else? Shopping?" she screeches.

"Here we go," Jimmy sighs. At the same time, Ivan says, "fuckin' women," and I say, "oh my god."

"Oh, you'll be saying 'oh my god' alright! Then he'll leave before you even wake up in the morning," she says with her hands on her hips.

I shake my head at her. "Sweetheart, I'm not sorry if he hurt your feelings because I know he tells his women the score before they jump into his bed. If you couldn't handle that, then you shouldn't have jumped. So please, stop embarrassing yourself and move on."

Grabbing the handles of the cart, I ignore what I was learning about brown beans in tomato sauce versus brown beans in molasses and swerve around the crazy lady with the black hair and scratchy voice. Thank shit she stayed put stunned in silence because I didn't want to listen to her anymore.

"Where in the ever-loving fuck do you find them, Jimmy?" I ask.

"Frank's. Sometimes The Pretty Kitty," he nonchalantly says.

"Good lord my friend, if you're going to The Pretty Kitty you must be running out of options," I say. He bumps my shoulder. "Hey don't knock it. They have new owners now and the place is like a classier gentleman's club. It's nice."

Looking behind me where we left the crazy black-haired woman I point over my shoulder and say, "Hunny, there was nothing classy about what we left in the brown bean isle."

Ivan laughs at our banter. "This is better than my big Russian family dinners. That's hard to top. Fuck, I might have to move to Canada."

Shaking my head at them both I keep walking. "C'mon, I just need meat now."

"Shit Jay could have sworn I heard Ryder give it to you this morning. You that hard up already?"

I answer with an elbow to the gut and keep walking.

With a smirk on my face.

***

I look around the picnic table at a bunch of satisfied faces. I forgot how much I missed cooking for people. This used to be the norm and the only people missing today were Laura, Brad and the kids.

Well, I shouldn't say the *only* people. My family would have been the ultimate dinner guests, but I'll settle for the new little family I have found. Ivan, Denny, Patrov, Jimmy and Ryder all sit around Jimmy's big oak table in the shop. The garage door is open to the rear, so I didn't have to loop around through the small man door with trays of food from the barbecue.

I decided on surf and turf and made steak Neptune with seasoned rosemary potatoes and a homemade Caesar salad. From the grunts, groans and little conversation I know the men are happy.

"Well fearless one, thank you for dinner it was excellent. But I have business I need to attend to." Patrov stands from his chair and moves around the table. He places a small kiss on the top of my head. I'm not sure what happened when he came to visit me in the infirmary, but since then it's like he has a newfound respect for me, and I treat him with the same.

"Anytime Andrei, I'm glad you enjoyed it."

Saying goodbyes to the rest of the men he exits through the front. Words of thanks come from all the men, and Ryder reaches under the table and gives my leg a squeeze. We haven't talked much since I got back, mainly because there have been people around and I was getting dinner ready, but I can see the guilt in his eyes for essentially making a poor judgment of me when it came to my relationship with Miller.

I tip my head to the side and he leans in, giving me a small kiss on the forehead. I catch Jimmy looking at me, sending me a wink, confirming that he did in fact have a talk with Ryder when we got back.

I really didn't need him to, but with a full belly, a few glasses of wine and a busy day with my new little family I'm content to let it go. Sometimes the glass is half-empty. Today it's half-full.

Grabbing the plate of leftovers, I set it down for Norma who lays down and savors the first real food she's had in a few days. By that I mean we have all been living on a lot of pizza and Chinese, so she's super happy about the beef and crab meat on her plate.

"Thanks Elle, that was delicious. Really," Denny says, Ivan nodding in agreement.

"No problem guys. I'm gonna start cleaning up." I begin to grab the plates and not to my surprise Ryder takes them from me and gives the other men what can only be described as *the look* before they too start clearing the table. I say nothing as I can't help the smirk on my face at how well they listen to him, even if the warning was not verbal.

I follow them up the stairs, only carrying the salt and pepper shakers, and watch as they all load the dishes in the dishwasher.

Setting the spices down on the stove, I watch them all head to their separate corners; Jimmy and Ivan at the island, Denny to the couch typing something on his phone. Ryder's arms come around my back. "Got a business call to make, beautiful. I'll be done in twenty, alright?" he says in my ear.

I nod my head. He kisses the top of it. "No worries."

I watch him head into the spare bedroom and close the door, while I head for a much-needed bathroom break.

Chapter Seventeen

I look down at the photo on my burner, not at all believing what I see, not sure what to do. I know what I *should* do but in the same thought I'm terrified to do it.

The photo that just came in is of Ryder outside Jimmy's shop, he's talking to Ivan and there is an 'X' drawn on his handsome face. Much like the pictures that painted Andrews wall in that horrific basement. Photos of me, all with an 'X' drawn on my face. We know how that turned out, so I know what it means this time; I also know that I have an important decision to make. I listen to the men talking out in the kitchen at Jimmy's. Ryder had a conference call with a client which he took in the spare bedroom. I appreciate the fact he is confidential about his work and I respect the fact that he needs privacy.

I power off my phone and put it in my pocket. Opening the bathroom door, making sure no one sees me I go into Jimmy's room and close the door behind me. I give Norma a decent hug, kissing her on her furry head where she lays on the end of Jimmy's bed. "Love you pretty girl, be good."

My fourteen-hole black Doc Martens are still where I left them. I waste no time putting them on. I'm already dressed in my ripped, dark skinny jeans and a long sleeve, loose black top. Once my boots are on, I slide the window open and climb out onto the fire escape. It's about twenty feet above the ground and the ladder goes down about ten feet to the side of the building where the gate is. I climb down, and let go when I reach the bottom rung, landing in a squat.

I take off at a run, down the side of the fence and cut through the neighboring business lot, and onto the next street. Once there, I turn right and head toward a place I never wished to go, at least not so soon.

I don't waste time letting my emotions get the best of me. I just keep running. It takes about ten minutes, and I have no doubt they have noticed I'm missing by now. Running toward the back of the house, I flip over the flagstone and get the key. Unlocking the back door to the garage I see my old girl. I wish I had more time to appreciate her black paint, and refurbished interior. I also wish I had the balls to step into the house my daughter and I once called home. Instead, I reach into the top drawer of the tool box and get the keys for my 1969 Chevelle. I grab the small knife out of the third drawer. It's not much, it's about four inches and had been left in the toolbox when my dad gave me the hand me down garage ornament. I stuff it in my boot, along with a screwdriver narrow enough that it looks like an ice pick.

I jump in my car and pray she starts, but I know Jimmy would have looked after her while I was gone. The engine purrs on the second try and I press the button on the visor to open the garage door. As soon as it's up enough, I put the car in drive and barely squeeze through before jetting out onto the street, toward the address I was given with the photo.

I think of a million different ways this could go. I calm my nerves a little, knowing I was given two hours to be where I was asked to go. I open the glove box and reach for the map inside. I don't have a smart phone, nor do I have a GPS on the shitty burner phone. I pull off the street and down another one that bypasses town and has the least number of houses on it.

Slowing down, I look at the map. The town I'm told to go is about fifty minutes from here, I just don't recognize the road name. I wasn't given the house number and I see that the road stretches for what looks to be about five miles in the country. Now that I have a general idea of where I'm going, I pull back on the road. I was told to text when I was close. I'm assuming I'll get the house number then.

Driving with a heavy heart, I think of Ryder. I know what I'm doing is right, and I hope he'll forgive me. I would never forgive myself if anything happened to him, and if there is more than just Andrew's brother in on this then it's possible someone has a gun trained on the building.

I laugh a little at the thought. *A fucking gun trained on the building?* When did my life become a Lifetime movie? In what normal person's life do people have guns—and I'm picturing a sniper rifle—trained on people unless they're in the middle of a war?

It's sad really that the paranoia is taking over, and I'm honest to shit worried that Ryder could lose his life to a bullet for all intents and purposes was actually meant for me.

Maybe I'm overthinking, and the 'X' on his handsome face was not meant to signify a bullet, but rather some other form of harm done to him. Either way it breaks my heart. He is such a good man, and he deserves nothing but good things. Things I hope to be able to give him, but that depends on what happens tonight.

It's past nine in the evening when I reach the road. I turn my phone back on and text the number given to me that I'm close. A bunch of texts and missed call alerts beep through but I ignore them for the one I'm looking for. The number 2273. Not wanting to be a complete idiot, I forward the texts to Cabe with the title *'I'm sorry'*. He'll know what I mean, and he'll be the quickest to figure it out. It also gives me a fifty-minute head start.

I leave the phone on but put it on silent and stash it under the seat. I don't want to be left out here to die and I know he'll be tracking me. I drive down the road which has now turned to gravel. I note that it's noisy, and I also note you can see headlights for miles. There is a forest to my left and to my right there are mostly fields, broken up between some remaining trees.

I pass a few country houses, a farm or two, and after a mile of seeing nothing, I come across my destination. It's set back from the road, with long grass that hasn't been cut in ages and a scattering of trees. I turn down the drive. There is a lone light on the porch that is past looking rugged but outright falling apart. The steps have caved in and there is a shutter hanging loose on the front. The house itself is not so poorly beaten; the paint is peeling on the wood sided home but it's fared better than the porch. There is a barn beyond that to the right, and a shed straight ahead. I see the shadow on the porch and park the car about thirty feet from the house and turn the ignition off, followed by the headlights. I don't miss the flash of steel at the man's side before he's once again cast in shadow.

Not knowing if I'm incredibly stupid or just plain fucking dumb, I get out of the car. I don't do it for myself. I do it for Ryder, for my family, for my friends who I wish no harm to come to. He walks into the house, not waiting for me. I'd find it odd but then again, I'm here, and it doesn't get any odder than that.

I'm here after all this time, wanting to know who the brother to Andrew is. I pray that I find out before I die. Or I pray that I'm able to kill him before he has the chance to hurt anyone I care about.

I take a wide step onto the porch, ignoring the broken boards that used to be called steps. There is a small light on inside the house and I see that it's not as shabby as the outside either. Its floors are filthy, and the decor looks dated, but it's held its shape.

I step into the home cautiously, ready to crouch and dig into my boot. Unfortunately, I don't get the chance before something heavy hits the back of my head, and I fall to the floor.

Chapter Eighteen

I feel warmth on the back of my neck.

Blood.

I'm cold and reminded of the last time I felt a similar sensation. I come to quickly, hating the feel of concrete under me. My heads hits the wall behind me and I let out a shocked cry at the pain, blinking my eyes a few times to regain full consciousness.

"Well hello, 'bout time you woke up. I was about to throw water on ya."

I freeze at the voice, wondering how life could be so cruel to me. Wondering how three times in a year I have found myself in a room filled with cold concrete and a man with evil eyes.

"What the fuck do you want, Braumer. And how'd you get my phone number?"

The useless bastard shakes his head at me, not at all pleased with my language but enjoying the banter.

"Ya had to give it when you were questioned at the station," he says, shaking his head. "Thought you could get away with it all, you worthless cunt, didn't you?"

I wiggle my wrists behind my back, coming to the conclusion they're zip tied. Harder to get off than rope but not as noisy as handcuffs would be.

Keep him talking.

"I don't know what you think it is I've gotten away with, I'm just wondering why you're here instead of the infamous twin brother."

Braumer's eyes light up.

Good.

"How do you know about him?" He leaves his position of leaning against an old table by the wall and storms in front of me, grabbing the front of my shirt and yelling in my face. "You know the little shit? Tell me!"

"I don't know who he is! I just know there were two of them! I told you that when the dead flowers were left on my porch!"

He looks into my eyes, his evil ones searching for the truth. He nods and let's go of my shirt, grabbing onto my hair instead.

"I put the fuckin' flowers there, a little way to let you know I was coming for you. Then ya went and took off! You thought you got away with it, killing him! I know you fucking done it! I know you did!"

I have no idea why he cares. "I'm not sure why the answer to that question is so important to you. Your retired, let it lie."

This earns me a backhand across the face.

"Let it lie? He was my fuckin' retirement plan! Him and that mental brother of his! Now what the fuck am I supposed to do? Huh? That bastard was *obsessed* with you, I've no idea why."

He paces back and forth in the basement and I do all I can to avoid the shakes that want to take over my body. "Well Braumer, pretty sure I'm here to die, aren't I? Might as well enlighten me because I have not one fucking clue what you're talking about."

He shakes his head. "Of course you don't you stupid bitch. Andrew knew how to play the stock market. Made a penny while he did it too. Not enough to show for, but he was waiting until he could find a way where he wouldn't get caught taking too much. I covered his ass for years, bailin' him out whenever he got caught buying blow down on Thirty Second Street. Had a temper too, but I got those assault charges dropped as well before his name had a chance to appear in the system." He proudly adds, "Looked after my boy, and he was gonna look after *me* until you went and fuckin' killed him! Now what do I got, huh? Shawn's useless, half-wit fuck that he is."

I'm reeling.

Stock Market.

Greed.

Looked after my boy.

Oh my god.

"You're their father? That makes no sense?"

He loses his temper, much like his evil son, and flings a chair across the room. "It fucking well does!"

I yell back. "You're their father? Yet they were abandoned at birth? I don't fucking believe it." I actually do get it, but I'll do anything to keep his mouth running.

Heavy footsteps head my way before he crouches down in front of me, his gut hanging over his pants. His breath smells of scotch and his balding head is covered in perspiration.

"Believe it. I hadn't been on the force too long before I met my Lucy," he sneers. Licking his filthy lips, he continues. "No good whore is what she was. Mother kicked her out for whatever reason, and she was running drugs to keep a roof over her head. Wrong place wrong time, and I taught her what it was like to be on the street. I taught her *real* good. She was in love too, some cook from a diner. I remember her beggin' me to stop 'cause they were gonna get mar-ried," he sing songs, shaking his head in disgust at the idea of matrimony, but not the insinuation of rape. "But I took one look at the sorry bitch and knew she was headed for a life of bein' a street rat.

"Every time I busted her, I had her. Never charged her for the drugs either. Once she started doin' them she was no fun, never screamed 'cause she was too high. Scrawny bitch. Ended up pregnant with my boys too. Fuckin' hell, eh?"

I swallow the vomit that's rising in my throat, wondering how someone can be so evil. I also let it run through my head that as much as I hate Andrew and all that he did, neither he nor his brother stood a chance in this life. Not with this man as an influence in their lives.

But he wasn't in Shawn's life, was he?

"Never got to raise my boys. Couldn't very well walk in to the hospital and announce myself the father of two kids to an underage fuckin' crack whore. Not me bein' a cop. Thought about adopting, but after Andrew went to his grandmother's I knew that bitch wouldn't roll over for me. Took one look at the other runt in the box fightin' for his life and wanted nothing to do with the kid. Doc said he'd be mental, not all there." He taps his head, "That ain't my boy."

This sick fuck doesn't deserve the air he breathes, and suffering the loss of my own child, one I would have loved no matter how she was born, makes me sicker. I can't hold it back. Leaning to the side, I vomit all over the floor. Braumer jumps back to avoid being covered in my sickness. I wipe my mouth on my shoulder and look up at the sorry excuse for a human being.

"You're sick. Leaving him is most likely the best thing you could have done for him, Braumer. But what of Andrew? What made him see your side of evil?" I tilt my head to the side, waiting for his answer.

"He was smart! That was my boy, the one you fucking killed! Shawn took off after that, not that the runt would get me any fucking money anyway. Kid's too fucking straight laced, but I'm teachin' 'em. That old foster woman made him the way he is. If she'd ever let him outta the house without her I woulda' got to him. But he was stuck on that old bitch like glue, little pussy that he is."

I'm trying my damndest to keep up with all the information. The blood running down the back of my head has slowed, but I'm still not one hundred percent. I hear a thud upstairs. Braumer whips a gun out of the waistband of his jeans and points it at me. I remain still, hoping like hell it's someone here to help, but at the same time hoping nobody gets hurt aside from the man in front of me.

"Don't move and don't fucking make a sound. You do, you're dead."

I already know I'm dead, but I don't tell him this. I watch his feet go up the stairs until they are no longer in my vision. As soon as he's out of site I arch my back trying to bring my arms down underneath my rear so I can pull them closer to my boots.

The tie is tight, so tight and higher up on my wrists than they should be. I wiggle, trying to move it lower when I hear a commotion upstairs followed by a thud. I struggle, bringing my legs up behind me but I hear footsteps start at the stairs. I give up and shove myself back into the upright position before he catches me reaching for the weapon, he doesn't know I have.

I see Braumer's feet first, followed by another set that seem to be more dragged than helped down the stairs. The legs are limp, barely co-operating.

"Got what you wanted I guess didn't ya, cunt? Here's who you've been tryin' to meet. Kid won't kill a damn grasshopper but thought he'd try and save ya by hittin' me in the head."

I watch as a smaller, more innocent version of Andrew is unceremoniously dumped on the floor. His clothes are a mess, his shirt is stained and he's skinny.

Shawn Flynn

He catches himself before his head hits the floor. His eye's look around frantically until they land on me. Pain and sadness turn into hope before they close, and he slumps the rest of the way to the floor.

I look for signs that he's hurt. His breathing is shallow, and his hair is mussed behind his temple suggesting Braumer whacked him the same as he did me.

"Stupid little shit. Shoulda' locked him in better," Braumer says, heading over to the table he was leaning against. It's more like a work bench among the cold concrete walls. I'm thankful there are no pictures of me here. Just a cellar-type basement in an old home. Shelves line the far wall with boxes of lord knows what. The rest is bare aside from the work bench.

Topping up the glass on the bench with what I assume is scotch from the smell on his breath, he turns around, glaring at me.

"What's he doing here? Out cold on the floor?" I ask.

He sneers back at me. "Wouldn't you like to know?"

I shake my head, letting him think that I've resigned to my fate. "You're going to kill me anyway, I know it. What's it matter if you tell me?"

As expected, he's happy to share his knowledge. Feeding off the fact that someone is listening to him. Loving he has all the attention he probably never got truthfully in his life because he's a useless sack of shit who nobody in their right mind would respect enough to listen to.

"Kid's along for the ride. Wasn't hard to get him either. As soon as my Andy told him he was his brother the little fuck lit up like a goddamn Christmas tree."

Setting the glass down he puts his hands out in front of himself, imitating a child in a whiny voice. "Oh, you're my brother! Oh brother can we play together! Can we? Can we!"

I don't bother hiding the look of disgust on my face at this sick man's rendition of the first time Shawn got to meet his brother. The first time a child who grew up in foster care found out he had living blood in the world.

Evil blood.

I gather from the way Braumer speaks that Shawn is not as far advanced as other people his age would be, perhaps developmentally challenged due to what he went through as an infant. The ice around my heart thaws a little on the side closest to him. If he is truly as Braumer makes him out to be, there is no way in hell he could have been involved in what happened to me. Maybe I'm wrong, but it just doesn't *feel* right. Not with the hope I saw in his eyes earlier, the lost eyes of a little boy who finally found what he wished for. The look of an innocent young man, albeit a grown up one.

The laugh of a madman pulls me from my thoughts. "Shoulda' seen 'em! Ah fuck, kid didn't know what to do with himself. Followed Andy around, did his homework for him. Readin' books 'n shit so Andy and me could work on the bigger picture. Even got 'em to sign his name on our business papers so if shit went south that stupid kid would take the fall and we'd be long gone." He sighs.

"Worked well too, 'til you fucked it all up. Told Andy he had no business with you, you were the same as the rest of 'em and his momma too. No good fuckin' whores. No clue why he wouldn't drop it. Dragged that half-wit around…"

"Enough!" I've had it, fucking had it! Who the hell treats their child with such disrespect?

He does, apparently.

"I would give anything, *anything* to have but five fucking minutes with my child. Whether bruised, broken or handicapped! She's my flesh and blood. Mine! What the hell is the matter with you?" I spit in his direction, not giving two fucks what he thinks of it. The glass he was holding shatters against the wall, its contents now gone. Heavy footsteps make their way toward me and he grabs hold of me by the arms, dragging my body up off the ground.

"Me?" His spit flies in my face as he speaks, the scent of scotch invading my nostrils. He shakes me, causing my head to snap back. "I'll tell you what the fuck's wrong with me—you! You're what's fucking wrong! I shoulda' been bookin' a flight to the sunny south right now! Livin' out my retirement with my boy and Honduran hookers! But no! I'm here because you went and killed my fuckin' boy!"

Letting go of my arms, he tosses me like a sack of potatoes against the work table. I hit my hip hard on the edge before I lose my balance and land on the floor, ass first. The pain shoots up my tailbone and I have no time to absorb it before he grabs me by the arms again, hauling me up, screaming in my face.

"It's all your fault! I had one last chance at retirement and you and that GI Joe of yours went and killed that too, splashin' Becker's name all through the mud! I only got half of what I was owed for getting you in jail and out of the way."

I've felt this way before, half-helpless and in pain. I hang onto the pain like I did last time, forgetting everything else but my fury and bring my right leg up to knee him in the balls. Braumer dodges to the right, and I end up hitting him slightly to the left in his upper thigh.

Grunting at the impact it only slows him down for a moment. My wrists crush between my body and the table and I try to push myself off again, a second attempt to get him down. Swinging my head forward I make contact with his nose, I watch the blood drip before I go to bring my leg up again. I'm not fast enough as his hand was behind his back, and he whips his gun out, smacking me in the side of the head with it. "Stupid cunt!"

I turn with the hit so it doesn't knock me out completely. I ignore the blood running out of my previously stitched eyebrow and turn around.

I won't give up, I can't.

My eyes don't meet his but the end of the barrel. In all the ruckus, I missed Shawn being helpless on the floor. I notice him now on his feet at the same time that Braumer does. Swinging the pistol from myself toward Andrew's brother, I launch forward. A deep howling, "No!" comes from Shawn's throat as I launch myself toward Braumer at the same time the gun goes off.

I don't know if it's the alcohol, or the adrenaline, but he catches me and himself before we hit the concrete floor. I'm shoved backward, pistol-whipped once again in the same motion. My back lands hard on the table.

"What that fuck is it with these two. Always after ya." He shakes his head.

I try to pull out of the fog, not from blood loss I don't think but from the third hit to my head in the past hour. I look in Shawn's direction. He's gasping for air, eyes pleading with me for help and holding onto his bloody chest. It's a high hold and I hope it's just his shoulder.

My head snaps back. Braumer has ahold of my hair and hauls me up off the table. I kick my legs out, but with hands behind my back, my balance is still off.

"You're gonna pay for that you bitch!"

He spins me around and elbows me hard in the back, forcing me down onto the table. Still gripping my hair, he forces my face into the hard, metal surface, sticky with scotch.

"They couldn't leave you well enough alone," his sick voice harps in my ear. "Don't know why, must have a golden fuckin' pussy. Won't know 'til I find out."

I kick my legs out behind me, trying to make contact with his shin, anything. Letting go of my hair, he grabs my bound wrists, pushing them up my back so my elbows are out. *The pain*! Fuck, the pain in my shoulders is excruciating.

"Arrrghhh," I howl low in my throat, not stopping with my legs.

"Scream. My Lucy screamed, nobody heard her and nobody will hear you either."

My arms cry out in pain and he uses his free hand to lift my head from the steel surface, slamming it back down again. I fight the stars behind my eyes, the blackness that wants to set in as he releases my hair. Then I hear the unmistakable sound of a zipper.

"No!" the grumbled plea leaves Shawn's mouth. Tears run down his cheeks and I watch as he tries to push himself off the floor to help. I know I will do whatever I can in this moment to keep him safe, he has no one. He has nothing. It's written all over the poor guys innocent face. He's just scared, and alone.

Except me. He has me.

I couldn't save Cory, I couldn't save my family, and I failed to save my daughter.

Redemption.

I use what little nails that are left on my hands and scratch at whatever flesh there is behind me. It's flabby, not firm. "You cunt!"

He jerks my arms up further. The popping sound echoing from my shoulder resonates through the room as he grabs hold of the back of my jeans. They're loose, due to my lack of eating properly. I curse myself for not wearing a belt.

"That useless fuck Stratus was supposed to send me videos! I didn't get any, but this will be much better."

The cries of Shawn fall into the background as my pants are pulled beyond my backside, the cool air of the basement evident on my bare skin. Still, I keep kicking.

Fight Elle, don't fucking stop. You keep fighting until he's down. And when he's down, you run. Run as fast as you fucking can!

Brock.

Brock.

I kick. With everything in me, I kick. I have no use of my arms. My head is too fuzzy and Shawn's pleas for Braumer to stop fall deaf in my ears. My struggle is futile. I feel his skin touching my thighs. I close my eyes, praying for the first time in my life for something, someone, anything that can help me.

"Gonna fuck ya," his sick voice says to the back of my head. "Then, I'm gonna fuckin' kill ya and that sorry excuse of a fuckin' kid."

I take a deep breath, not at all resigned to my fate. Not ready to succumb to what is about to happen.

Lilly.

Cory.

My parents.

I've been using my right leg for the past three attempts to kick him, not my left. My hip hurt too badly on that side. I relax my body, letting him think he's won. Perhaps he has? But I won't give up.

Never.

I lean further into the table, away from Braumer. I relax my body into it, letting him think I've passed out. I know when he comes to this conclusion because he pulls back, letting go of most of the pressure holding my arms up.

Stepping away from my body slightly, I hear the unmistakable sound of pleasure. Him getting himself ready. I hate to admit that I know he wasn't hard when he leaned into me, I also know he's over sixty. Probably doesn't happen as quickly as it used to.

THE UGLY ROSES

I listen. Only using my sense of sound, I get a feel for where he's at and bring my left foot up behind me, bending at the knee and forcing my foot upward. The following scream is like music. I lean up and dive to the side, falling hard on my ribs.

Braumer is on the floor, hands between his legs with face white. Bringing my legs up behind me I ignore the agony in my shoulder as I try to grab the knife out of my boot. My back screams in pain. My pants, still straddling my bare ass, hinders my movement but I push through. I touch the tip of it, just getting the top of the handle in my fingertips before he launches himself to the side, kicking my feet.

I lose the knife and it skids across the floor behind me. Rolling to the side, I get it back in my hand, but not before he lands on top of me.

"You fucking bitch! You'll pay for that!"

He backhands me once again across the face. I don't know how many more hits I can take before the lights go out. I'm also sickened by the fact he's sitting on top of me when my pants are below my ass and his flaccid cock is hanging from his.

I gag, attempting to roll to the side so I can vomit. Grabbing hold of my throat he stops the process, sucking the life out of me. He lowers his face, close, too close to mine. I try to bring my knee up again but I can't; my pants and his weight limit the impact.

I gasp, trying desperately to suck air into my lungs.

"You're dead, cunt."

The sick, evil smile is one of the last things I see before his body goes flying through the air. I try to reach for my throat but I can't, my hands are still tied.

Literally.

I cough, and roll to the side, vomit coming from my mouth. I feel the binds being cut as I watch a flurry of black in front of me. I watch blood spray against the cold concrete walls as my eyes water, blurring everything in front of me.

The feeling of someone's hands on my bare legs makes me jolt. "No!" I gurgle through my sickness before the distorted vision of my Viking settles in front of my face. I move my arms to pull up my jeans, howling in pain through my tears.

"Easy girl, it's me, it's Denny, babe," he says while holding his hands between us.

I can't help the sob pushing through my tears.

"I'm gonna cover you up Elle, not gonna touch you alright?"

I knew as soon as it was him he wouldn't hurt me, but I have a hard time nodding my foggy head.

"O-oh-okay," I manage to say since my head won't cooperate. I feel his hands, gentle on my legs as he pulls my jeans up over my hips. My hands lie limp at my side, my shoulder too sore or dislocated to move. I allow my sight to focus across the room. I see another man grabbing under Shawn's shoulders, trying to drag him away.

"Noooooo!" I wail as best I can. "D-d-don't hurt him!"

Denny leans in low to my face. "Elle, what's going on?"

I shake my head slightly, so close to passing out but not ready to until I see that Shawn is okay. "Don't hurt him," I whisper. "He's good, he tried to save me. Please don't hurt him."

THE UGLY ROSES

The last thing I remember is Viking blues, sincere, intent, and promising.

Chapter Nineteen

Beep...

Beep...

Beep...

The sound of the heart monitor machine is my awakening, and a firm reminder that I am in fact alive. The sickening smell of disinfectant and antiseptic invades my nostrils as I fight to open my eyes.

They feel glued shut and my body as though it weighs a ton. I can't move my feet, or at least I don't think I can, and I struggle to move my fingers next. The beeping of the heart monitor quickens as I fight unconsciousness and my non-cooperative body.

"Shhhhh." Ryder whispers followed by his thumb caressing my cheek, then between my eyebrows as he calms the frown most surely on my face. "Calm beautiful, you're okay."

His soft words spoken against my temple do just that, calm me.

So, I go back to sleep.

***

"She's coming out of it Mr. Callaghan. We never know how long this process takes because every patient is different. Some people can suffer a head injury and be awake in a day or two. Sometimes it takes weeks, even months. The swelling has decreased rapidly the past few days. However, it could be the emotional trauma that has kept her in a comatose state."

Shuffling sounds fill the room, someone moving back and forth. "I just feel fucking useless, Doc. It's been a week."

"Give her time. Talk to her, it's all you can do."

The door closes and a warm hand grabs mine. I know those fingers, those callouses. They're familiar yet not as I feel what I think is a bandage.

"I used to watch you late at night." Ryder whispers, "Fuck that sounds creepy, but I don't mean for it to. I have trouble sleeping, or I did until I slept with you. Not because of nightmares like the ones you've suffered from. I can't really tell you why because I don't know. Maybe I just needed you because you seemed to fix that problem."

He sighs and I feel his warm breath on my hand. "So when I couldn't sleep at night, I'd sit on the balcony outside my room and I'd see you. You'd sit in the same spot for hours, watching the water and laying on that big red lounge of yours on your back porch. It was hard to make out your facial expressions from that far away and it drove me insane because I wanted to know what was going on in that pretty stubborn head of yours."

Warm lips touch the back of my hand and he continues to hold it to his face, speaking against it.

"I couldn't get enough of you and you wanted nothing to do with me. That was a hard hit for a man like me because I've never wanted for anything when it came to women; it's always been easy. Until you that is. You challenged me beautiful, and as much as I wanted to let my dominant streak through, I knew if I did, you'd run. You *did* run.

"You pushed me away, and as much as I wanted to fight for you, I still treated you like a leaf on a tree in the fall. If I set you off, I knew all it would take is one more gust of wind to send you flying. I couldn't take that chance because I needed more of you. I still want more of you. I want all of you—every piece that you'll share with me."

I feel the wetness on my hand that I can only imagine is tears. "I thought you were dead, beautiful. Fuck! Jimmy drove so goddamn fast to get to that house Braumer had you in. I was so pissed off you did that! I'm still pissed off because all I could think was that the last time I spoke to you it was to say I had a business call I needed to make, not that I loved you. All I could think about was the mundane useless shit I didn't get to do with you yet. Like wake up with you again or take you out for dinner because I'm a prick who hasn't taken his woman out on a proper date yet. It all just flooded in because I thought it would be too late to save you and you'd be gone before I got to do that. Before I got to find out what your favorite color is, your favorite memory as a child or what made you decide to name your daughter 'Lilly'. I want to know all of that and more, I need all of you, Elle. So wake up beautiful, please wake up."

The hitch of his breath, the gruffness in his voice and the wetness on my hand breaks my heart.

I did this to him.

I put myself here to protect him, but I rendered him to be what he is now—a broken man crying beside my bed. I try to move, I try to open my eyes, but it doesn't happen. I let him hold my hand, palm to his cheek as he rests his head on the mattress. I lay silent, listening to his breathing, feeling it on my wrist.

Time passes.

THE UGLY ROSES

I'm not sure how long but it's darker. My eyelids aren't as bright, so I try again to open my eyes. The first small sliver of light filters through but it's muted. There is a light on somewhere behind me and the light in what I think is the bathroom is on. Everything's a little blurry, so I blink again, trying to clear my vision.

The beige walls are boring, the white curtains and bedding all blur together and I look down, taking in the form of Ryder, his head pointed in my direction. His knuckles are swollen. His right hand is wrapped so I'm assuming it's worse than the left one. There's a small bruise on his left cheekbone and a few scrapes, but other than that he's as handsome as the first day I saw him.

I look at my hand, still resting on his cheek where he holds it to his face. His stubble has grown almost into a beard now. It looks to be about a week's worth of growth on his handsome face. I will my fingers to move, watching them, trying to force them into motion. My thumb twitches first, followed by the rest of my fingers. One by one, they move, and I lightly caress his face, moving my fingers down his beard, causing his hand to fall limp on the bed.

The pads of my fingers brush over his lips and black eyes meet mine, beautiful, glowing black eyes with silver around the outside and an unshed layer of moisture waiting to fall down his cheeks. He pulls my fingers tight against his mouth and kisses them. I close my eyes, overcome with emotion, so grateful for the strong man at my bedside.

"Wake up beautiful, show me those beautiful green eyes; I missed them."

Opening my eyes, I let the emotion escape, cascading down my cheeks so that we mirror each other. I've never seen a grown man cry, and it's my undoing. I try to reach for him with my left arm and let out a small cry of pain. Strong hands frame my face and he presses his lips to mine.

137

"Shhh, beautiful. Don't move. Your shoulder was reset but you have a small fracture in your humerus bone." I kiss him back, lightly because every part of my face hurts. "I missed you beautiful, fuck did I miss you."

"Missed you too. Lay with me Ry."

He pulls back a fraction, eyes moving over every part of my face before he responds. "Nothing else is broken, but it might hurt your arm if I move you over. I'll be careful, okay?"

I simply nod and he moves his strong arms under me, sliding me gently across the bed. Kicking off his boots he climbs in slowly, putting his arm under my head, turning me toward him.

Our heads are only a few inches apart as he lays on his side, touching my face, my hair, my arm. All gentle, all Ryder. It's like he's reassuring himself I'm here, that I'm okay. I allow him to and only using my eyes I do the same to him. Taking everything in and memorizing every feature.

"How long have I been out?" I ask, my voice hoarse due to lack of use. He holds a cup to my mouth with a straw and I'm grateful for the cool liquid.

"Eight days. Longest week of my life, beautiful." I can see it was the longest week, he looks tired, the lack of shaving a sure sign he hasn't been looking after himself.

"I'm sorry," I tell him.

"What happened to 'I'm sorry is an admission of guilt?' You're not guilty of anything beautiful, I'm just happy you're awake. "Shaking my head, I reply, "but I am guilty. I brought you here Ryder. I made the choice to go out there on my own. I know it was stupid, but I can't say I would do it differently next time. My main concern in all of this was not letting anyone else close to me get hurt, please tell me no one got hurt?"

Running his hands through my hair, he tells me, "Everyone's fine, beautiful. Except for Shawn, he's still…"

"Oh my God! Tell me!" I whisper yell after rudely cutting him off.

He gives me a small smile, "Shawn's fine. He's down the hall, his first surgery went well but a day later he started to bleed internally. They got in and fixed it. Now he's resting up. He won't talk much to anyone other than the nurses. They said he keeps asking for someone, they don't know who it is but then he just says, 'the girl who saved my life.' He wants to speak to you, Elle. Detective Miller tried to talk to him, but it didn't go very far. He's shy, he's developmentally challenged, and this place is new to him. Plus, he doesn't know anyone here but he seems to know you, or trust you enough to want to speak to you."

I still don't know who he is, or how he knows me, but I know I need to talk to him. "Can you take me?"

"Not tonight beautiful, it's two in the morning and I just got you back. We'll go first thing in the morning, okay?"

I nod my head, silently answering him and closing my eyes. They're too heavy to keep open. I take a deep breath, asking the question I'm not sure I want the answer to. "Braumer?"

Ryder's arms come around me, his lips settle in my hair. "He's gone. Nobody can hurt you anymore, now sleep, beautiful."

I relax into his warmth, wanting to fight sleep in favor of more answers, but at the same time feeling safe has never felt so good.

HARLOW STONE

I forgot what it felt like.

So, I let it all go in Ryder's arms, and actually sleep without fear for the first time in over a year.

Chapter Twenty

"You look much better, Ms. O'Connor. I'm going to book you for one last CT scan to make sure there's no more swelling or any other concerns in your brain. But if all goes well, which I think it will, you can go home."

Home.

"Thank you, Dr. Maxwell," I say, nodding absently because I get to go *home.* I know that's not here, I also don't know if that's possible after the judge ordered me to stay close. I don't know anything that's happened regarding Andrew's death, or me killing him.

I know nothing and I haven't asked because I haven't had time. As soon as my eyes were open this morning the doctor was here, and now I watch as he goes out the door, prepared to ask Ryder a million questions but wanting to see Shawn more. He might be the answer to a lot of my questions.

"I'm ready, Ryder. Take me to see Shawn, please?"

"Do you want to wait to see the nurse?" he asks.

I shake my head, ignoring the pounding. "No, I want to go now."

Placing a hand on my arm he says, "Elle, you have a catheter in, and it's attached to the bed. Not sure I can take that out for you, beautiful. So, either you wait, or I wheel you down there in the bed."

I waste no time answering, nor do I think about being embarrassed. "Bed, just get me there Ryder, I need to see him."

Denny chooses this moment to walk in. "See who?" he asks.

"Shawn," both Ryder and I answer at the same time.

Denny sets a box of pastries down on the table along with a tray of coffee before placing a light kiss on my head. Jesus, I love him. Looking over my face with sad eyes he says, "Nurse had him up and walking, and he talked to me a bit yesterday. I'll see if I can get him down here."

I give him a weak smile. "Thank you, Denny, for everything. But if you're not back here in five I'm coming down there." He knows I'm not joking, I also know he won't let me down.

Four minutes later, a bright-eyed Shawn is wheeled into my room. He looks better than he did in the basement. His dirty clothes are gone, and he looks freshly showered. His arm is in a sling and I see bandages through the top of his hospital gown. I thought he looked like a younger Andrew, but he looks nothing at all like him because his eyes are so *happy*. They glow. Like a child opening up a present on Christmas day. He radiates light and all things good in this world.

"Gina!" he says with a huge smile on his face. I feel the fog, and then the clarity as what he called me sets in.

"Oh my god," I whisper as goosebumps pebble my flesh.

Ryder grabs my hand. "What's wrong, Elle?"

I look at him briefly through watery eyes, and back again at Shawn.

Shawn?

"Gina, it's me! It's Matty! I'm so glad you're okay, Gina!"

I shake my head, my recently swollen brain overcome with a million memories.

"Counselling on Campus, this is Gina speaking. How may I help you today?"

"Hi Gina. It's Matty again. I asked for you specifically, I hope that's okay?"

Ah, Matthew. He's one of the sweeter ones that call. The guy sort of reminds me of the slightly dorky kid in school that gets a bad rap, but he's actually incredibly sweet and very intelligent.

"Oh my god. Shit!" I blink toward the ceiling, willing the tears at bay.

"Talk to me Elle, what the fuck is going on?" Ryder grates out as he exchanges a look with Denny.

"Bad words!" Matty shouts.

I look to the innocent, developmentally challenged man in the wheelchair. Swallowing the lump in my throat I say, "Matty. You used to call me a lot at Counselling on Campus?"

A bright smile takes over his face. "Yup! That was me Gina! I knew you'd remember me! Andrew said you would never remember me, but I knew you would!"

I close my eyes at the mention of my nightmare's name. Ryder puts his hand to my back, rubbing small circles and I'm sure he's completely confused as to what we are talking about.

"It's nice to meet you, Matty. I have a few questions I'd like to ask you, is that okay?"

He nods his head. "I'm just happy you're okay, Gina. I'm so sorry for what Andrew and his Dad did. I tried to stop him

143

Gina, I really tried but he was too heavy! I tried to stop him I promise!"

I put out my hands, motioning for him to calm down. "It's okay Matty. I know you tried. It's okay."

Unshed tears linger in his eyes, but he shakes his head.

"Matty, do you know what happened to me before? What happened to your brother?"

His happy face is gone, and a few tears fall down his cheeks. "Andrew said we needed to protect you. You were my friend first but he said I had to help him take pictures, so we knew that you'd be safe, Gina. He said someone wanted to hurt you and I didn't want anyone to hurt you 'cause you were so nice. People weren't always nice to me, but you were always nice, Gina."

He sniffles a little, so I reassure him. "It's okay Matty, you can tell me. I'm not mad at you, okay?"

Sweet, brown eyes meet mine and he continues. "Andrew always called you Jayne and said that the name you used at counselling on campus was a fake name. Is that true, Gina?"

"It is true, Matty."

"Can I still call you Gina?"

I nod my head. "You sure can Shawn." This earns me a small smile.

"I like Matty, all my friends call me Matty."

I nod my head. "Matty it is."

Shawn Matthew Flynn

THE UGLY ROSES

I watch the shadows come back over his face as he speaks. "Andrew wasn't so nice to me Gina. He told me I had to help him get you, so we could protect you from the bad people. But after I helped him, he put me in a room and told me I couldn't come out because then the bad people would find me too. He told me I had to be really quiet. But I heard you scream, and I knew the bad man found you so I came out of my room but it was Andrew being a bad man, and he was dragging your little girl's dad down the stairs. He told me he was helping him, but I knew he wasn't because he looked so *mean*, Gina. He told me to run and hide, before anyone else found me too and I ran, Gina. I ran and I didn't help." He's sobbing now, and I reach out and grab his hand, trying to soothe him. He doesn't fully understand.

"A-An-Andrew taught me how to drive but I'm not very good. He told me if I got caught, I could get in trouble so not to drive in town. But he gave me a driver's license just in case. So, I drove the van so I could get to town and I bought a bus ticket to the cabin. Andrew said it would be our hiding place if the bad man came. So, I went there so I could hide but you weren't okay, I didn't know but you weren't okay Gina, and I was scared."

I rub the back of his hand. "It's okay Matty, and it's not your fault."

"But it is, Gina! I should have been braver! Andrew and his dad were the bad man, but they lied! Miss Marion told me lying's not good and they lied, Gina! Brothers aren't 'spose to lie!"

Not giving two fucks about my catheter or the tubes in my arm I slide to the edge of the bed, ignoring the pain shooting up my arm and embracing the broken young man in front of me. I rock him a little to the side, and back again.

"It's okay Matty, we're both okay."

He continues to cry guilty tears into my hospital gown, a broken young boy in a grown man's body.

He breaks.

"I don't want to help them anymore, Gina," he sobs. "Andrew's dad tried to get me to show him how Andrew does computer stuff, but I don't know all of it and I don't want to show him. He's *mean* Gina, and if I'm not fast enough he gets mad and locks the door on me. Don't make me go back there. I'm sorry Gina, please don't make me go back there."

Swallowing past the lump in my throat, I respond, "I never make a promise I can't keep. I promise you Matty, you will never, ever go back to a bad man ever again. I promise."

***

"Matty, can I ask you something?"

After this morning, Ryder had Cabe dive into more work. One, being tying all the loose ends together after Matty gave us information, and two being working out what we can do for Matty after he's out of the hospital.

It's now dinner time and Ryder had Denny bring in food for the four of us. We're eating in a common room down the hall and so far I have learned that Matty loves to cook mac and cheese, he loves animals, and up until this point he has survived pretty much on his own with a little help from Andrew along the way.

I didn't remember all of our conversations from when I worked at Counselling on Campus, but Matty said when he told me he got a donation to his scholarship, which was for his studies on working with animals through a special program for developmentally challenged kids, it was from his old foster parent, Marion Downey.

He said he never got to finish his studies because Andrew persuaded him to enroll in computers instead, ultimately helping Andrew and Braumer in their end goal to make dirty money. But Matty just wanted to help his brother and did whatever he said to do; including putting the dirty company in Matty's name, they even let him name it—*ANIG Tech Solutions*, a palindrome of Gina, one of the nicest people he spoke to.

"We're friends Gina, you can ask me anything."

I smile. "We are friends, Matty. I was just wondering how you've lived this past year with Andrew gone. Do you have some help?"

He shakes his head, eating another mouthful of chicken-fried rice. "Sometimes Mrs. Davenport brings me supper. She lives across the hall."

"That's nice Matty, but I mean do you have a *job*? Who pays your rent?"

"I walk dogs four days a week, so that helps my groceries. And I pay the rent now. Five hundred and sixty dollars a month, but sometimes Mr. Wickens makes us pay extra when it's cold outside because he says we use too much of the heater."

"Matty, who's 'us'?"

"Me and Andrew. Andrew helped me get the apartment, but then Andrew left and it's just me and I don't have a lot, but I know where he hides the money because I saw him do it when he thought I was asleep on the couch. So I just use it to pay the rent and stuff," he says, shrugging like it's no big deal to pay rent out of a box of hidden cash every month.

"I thought the house I was in was Andrew's house, Matty?"

He nods. "Yup, it was. And the cabin, *and* the apartment. Andrew said he liked lots of places to sleep. But he told me not to tell his dad about the apartment and the cabin because it was our secret."

I look to Ryder and he nods his head toward Matty. I know what he wants so I ask, "Matty, are you allowed to tell me where your apartment is?"

"Will you come and visit me?" he asks excitedly.

I nod with a smile. "I would love to come and visit you, Matty."

He smiles back. "I live at five-three-two West Palmer Street, Unit 3-B."

I frown. "That's not a very good area Matty, maybe when we get out of here, I could find you a new place to stay? Maybe somewhere where the people are nicer?"

His ears perk up. "Maybe somewhere with pets? Can I get a dog? I've always wanted a dog, but Mr. Wickens won't let us have pets."

"Yes Matty, somewhere where you can have a dog."

I fight the tears behind my eyes at something so simple, yet incredibly huge to him. I watch as Ryder removes himself from the table, most likely calling Cabe, pointing his men to Matty's apartment to see what they can find. I don't move from my spot beside my new friend, grateful that he's the kind human being he is, resenting myself for fearing him for the past year.

Of course he'll never know what I thought of him, but I'll spend the rest of my life giving him the respect he deserves and being the friend he never had.

Chapter Twenty-one

Ryder

I watch as Elle looks at herself in the mirror. Once again her face is a mess of bumps, bruises and stitches. Her left eye is half swollen shut, her cheekbone twice the size it should be. Her temple and forehead have a long cut; fifteen stitches in total. She'll have a scar, and if it bothers her, I'll find the best doctor in the country to fix it.

I put my hands on her bare shoulders in the hospital bathroom and kiss the back of her neck. "It'll fade, beautiful. Not sure about you but I'm just happy you're here, bruises and all."

She leans into my touch and I move her toward the shower. I've already shed my clothes, against hospital policy I'm sure but no way in fuck was I letting someone else wash my woman. I'm perfectly capable and more than happy to do so.

Guiding her under the spray, I make sure she stays far enough out that it won't hit her face. I take care of washing her from top to toe. I don't wait for her to be embarrassed, nor do I give her another option as I sit her down on the stool in the shower and shave her legs.

Elle's always looked after herself, and I know it probably bothers her not to be able to do this on her own. I also know she won't ask for help because she's too damn stubborn. So I had Laura bring whatever Elle would need when she came to visit today. Now here I sit, shaving the love of my life's legs and not giving one fuck what anyone thinks about it.
I love her legs, and every other part of her.

"Tell me what happened in the basement Ryder, after I passed out. You guys were beating around the bush today, but Laura told me there were reporters outside the hospital. She also told me there's been a flurry of activity in and out of Jimmy's shop. I've given you all day and you haven't brought it up. But I need to know. With details Ryder, I need to know because I find it odd that I haven't been questioned by the cops since I woke up. The doctor didn't even mention them being here."

I blow out the breath I was holding. "Cops will be in Elle, but I asked them to give you some time." She gives me a look. I knew this was coming. I don't want to talk about it, but she deserves the truth. She deserves it all. She's the one who lived in fear for so long and she deserves to know how that fear ended.

So I tell her, letting out what happened from the time I left Jimmy's apartment to the time I left the basement.

"The window's open, she went out the fire escape!"

I don't bother looking at the open window; instead I jog down the steps to Jimmy's shop, calling Cabe on the way.

"Boss," he answers.

"Track Elle's phone, where is she?"

I jog out the back door to my SUV, Denny, Ivan and Jimmy on my heels.

"No signal Boss, last tower ping was from where you are now."

"Fuck!" What the hell has she done? Why the fuck would she leave?

"Keep on it Cabe, call me the minute it gets back on!"

I stop at the SUV and face Jimmy. "Where would she go?"

THE UGLY ROSES

He paces for a minute. "Only place she ever went was the cemetery, but usually when it's dark and she always took Norma. She's not there if Norm's here. I'd say she got a wild hair and went to Franks or her old home but that 'aint right either. Let's do a drive by there but I know I'm not wrong, just don't want to rule it out."

We all hop in my SUV, driving at breakneck speed toward her old home first since it's on the way to Franks. Jimmy points to the left, then right before we end up on a small street where the lawns are kept clean and the houses are looked after.

The kind of place you raise a family.

"Fuck," he says.

"What? Talk to me Jimmy."

"Her fucking car's gone. Shit, this is not good."

I slam my hand on the steering wheel. "Little more explanation would be good!"

"It's her car, the-fuckin'-car. Her dad found it for her. She hasn't driven it since the attack. 1969 Chevelle. If she got in that car she was in a fucking hurry. Never even closed the garage door. I'm telling you, it's not good."

I turn in the driveway, hopping out I yell to Jimmy, "you drive!"

Jimmy pulls back onto the road, heading back the way we came. "What do we know Ivan? Denny? C'mon guys think of something. What about that fuck's house? Is it still there? In his name?"

Jimmy shakes his head. "Not in his name, run down and been for sale since the attack. Nobody will buy it."

Can't say I blame them.

We drive toward town, hoping, waiting for Cabe to call. We make a loop past the cemetery just in case, but she's not there. We knew she wouldn't be, but I couldn't just sit on the side of the road and wait.

Thirty minutes later my phone rings. "Tell me you got news."

"Just forwarded the address to your phone. Keep heading in the direction you're going for ten more miles and turn north when you hit highway twenty-one. Elle got a text to her phone. She just forwarded it to me and wrote 'I'm sorry'. It's a picture of you boss, with a big 'X' on your head."

"Fuck!" I bash my fist on the dash.

"She was told to head to Haraldson, and that she had two hours to get there. Once she got there, she was forwarded the house address. I have screen shots of her texts. You're about thirty-five minutes behind her from where you are now. House address is on your phone, drive fast boss and you'll make it in twenty. I don't feel good about this. At all."

"That makes a fucking truck full of us." Grunts and groans and a few curses agree with me as I disconnect from Cabe. I don't need to tell him to stay on it—he knows.
"Where's the nearest law enforcement detachment from there, Jimmy? You familiar with the area?"

"We drove past one five minutes ago. Haraldson doesn't have its own; nearest major town on the other side of that would be thirty minutes away, at least. It's not so much a town, just a name."

I curse, hating this fucking place already. One minute, I'm in a city at court. Fifteen minutes out you're in a smaller town, and then boom you're in a fucking cornfield. Thankful for the straight paved highway, we top out the speedo on the SUV at a hundred and fifty, hoping to hell livestock doesn't decide to cross the highway, but prepared to plow through to get my woman.

"Left in two, boss."

I nod over my shoulder at Ivan, thankful he's paying attention and Jimmy makes the turn. This road is gravel, so he slows down, watching the numbers pass by until we come closer to our destination.

***

I don't know how Maverick pulls this shit off. My ghost of an employee always manages to keep us hooked up wherever we go. I pull the two glocks out from underneath my seat and watch my men do the same. Jimmy doesn't have a gun, nor do I know if he knows how to shoot one. He's also not as trained as we are, but I hand him one of my own.

"Know how to shoot?"

He pulls the clip out, checks the safety and holds it comfortably as we edge up the driveway toward the house. Two flank left, Ivan and I take the right.

I note my woman's badass car in the driveway, but nothing else. There's a shed and a barn in the distance, but with the only light coming from the house we head there first. I take the back, looking in the windows, closing in on the door.

"Noooooo!" a male voice from inside wails, and Ivan and I waste no time, bursting through the back door as Denny and Jimmy come in the front. I hear a thump come from below and search for the stairs. Ivan rushes through, opening up the door

and I charge ahead, not at all prepared for what I'm about to see, but willing to kill.

Elle is lying on the ground, blood pouring from her forehead, eye swelling shut, pants down to her knees and Detective fucking Braumer has his hands around her throat.

"You fuck!" I roar, moving my gun to my left hand and grabbing him by the back of my shirt with my right. I toss him across the room, and he lands with a smack against the concrete. It's not enough; I want to hear bones break. I want to hear flesh rip.

I need to make him bleed.

I need to make him suffer.

I ignore the half-limp male body on the floor, watching as Ivan tries to haul him up. I briefly register my woman yelling 'no', but all I see is red.

All I smell is death.

"Get her outta here, Denny." I say quietly, among the chaos and heavy footsteps. I'm surprised he heard me but I watch him lift her gently and carry her up the stairs.

I put my gun in the back of my pants.

I don't need it, not for him.

I notice a knife on the floor, old and rusted. "That was Gary's. I work on Elle's car. It's been in the toolbox he gave her for years," Jimmy says.

Fitting, I think.

Gary O'Connor deserves justice, as does Elle, her mother, and her daughter. This is the fuck who has caused her pain, and what better way to return that than with an old, rusty knife.

The duller, the better.

Braumer scrambles along the floor, his gun is about six feet away but Jimmy kicks it with his boot to the other side of the room. I look to Ivan, watching as he hauls Andrew's brother in a fireman's carry and takes him up the stairs, nodding at me as he goes.

Respect.

Understanding.

Loyalty.

I'd tell Jimmy to go too, but that's his call.

I watch the unfit fuck lose purchase a few times before he finally gets to his feet, pulling his pants up along the way. "Move out of my way, or I'll have you arrested!"

For the first time since Elle went missing, I laugh. How the fuck could I not?

"You're not a cop anymore Braumer. So tell me, who's going to come in here and save your ass after you tried to rape and kill my woman?"

"It's my word against yours!" he shouts.

I shake my head in a condescending way. "No, it's your word against Callaghan Security and an alive and breathing good woman. But you won't be around for that, so really it's just our word."

I haul back and punch the prick in the side of the head. Not hard enough to knock him out, or at least I hope not. I'd like to play for a while if I can keep the rage at bay. I watch as he stumbles to the right, loving the sight of dried blood beneath his nose because I know Elle fought back. He grabs the steel bench to regain his balance before standing back up and I notice the angry, red scratches on his arms. I know that Elle's hands were tied behind her back and it can only mean that it happened when he held her down. Not being able to contain the fury, I grab him by the back of the shirt and slam his head down on the table.

"Tell me you sick fuck, tell me what you did to my woman. Might make me kill you faster."

"Fuck you!"

Grabbing his left hand, I yank it up behind his back, twisting and pulling from the thumb.

"Agghhhh!" he screams as I jab my elbow in his spine. He brings his right hand up, trying to push off the table and I drive the knife down into it until it hits the steel.
"Tell me!"

"Agghhh! I was gonna kill her! She killed my boy! She killed him, she deserves to die!"

I pull the knife out of his hand and haul him up, spinning him around so his ass is against the table. Jimmy flies in from my right, slamming the cocksucker in the head with a punch that would make any man proud. He comes back with his left, nailing him in the ribs and follows through with an upper cut to the jaw.

Braumer slumps down off the table, falling to the floor on his knees.

"You were gonna kill her. Why rape her? You get off on shit like that? Women who don't want to be touched? Or are

you just so hard up you can't find someone to give it to you?" I growl.

He spits a mouth full of blood on the floor, coughing through his response. "Figured she must have had a golden pussy. Andrew was obsessed with her and the other one thinks she's a fuckin' angel or somethin'. She thinks she can get away with killin' my boy? I was teachin' her! No good, fuckin' whore deserved to be put in her place after what she did!"

I bend down, wishing I could drag this out longer but for the first time, I'm not able to check the fury.

I can't keep the rage at bay.

"Know what I do to people like yourself, Braumer?"

I watch his eyes go wide as I reach out to him.

He doesn't get a chance to answer.

Some people say it sounds like a snap, some say it sounds like a pop. Either way, the feeling of someone's neck breaking under my bare hands has never felt so satisfying.

Chapter Twenty-two

Elle

I sit, dumbfounded listening as Ryder finishes his side of what happened last week. "After that, Jimmy nailed me in the face, twice. He said it was so it looked like I put up a fight, he's not wrong, it did. But I let him do it Elle, because that man loves you, and if it weren't for me what happened in jail wouldn't have happened. That's on me, and I have to live with that."

I watch as he takes the towel from the hook, we're both long past wrinkled from the shower and he wraps it around my body where I still sit on the stool. After wrapping one around his waist, I grab his hand, silently asking him to help me stand up which he does.

I don't let him lead me out of the bathroom. I wrap my one good arm around his body and kiss his heart, keeping my eyes on his as he looks down at me.

"I've tried. So hard I have tried to figure out how to say something that meant more than those three small words. Because they are small, and they don't at all encompass the depth and meaning of what I want to say to you. I can't come up with something else, maybe because I'm not articulate enough, maybe because there are only ways to show you but no other words. For now, all I come up with for words is nine of them, I love the fuck out of you Ryder Callaghan. You're an incredibly amazing man and those words are still too small, but there they are. One day, when I'm not so beat up and fractured, I'll show you how much I mean them."

Shock.

Envy.

Longing.

Love.

All of those and perhaps many other emotions cross his face before his lips touch mine.

"You already do, beautiful. You already do."

***

Walking through the front door of Ryder's house is surreal to say the least. It's been two weeks since I was attacked by Detective Braumer, and while in his basement I would have never guessed that two weeks later, this is where I would be.

Many things were cleared up over the past few weeks, and as much as I'd like to know all that had happened, I decided to let go of a little baggage and allow Ryder to carry it for me.

I learned some things, mostly from Matty. Shawn Matthew Flynn, to be exact. He told me hours' worth of stories, from his time in foster care to his time with Andrew. I learned when he was forced to ditch his dream of working with animals in order to help Andrew with computer science assignments, he came across the number for Counselling on Campus. Andrew did most of the work but not surprisingly Matty is well taught when it comes to the computer. Sometimes he got upset when he couldn't perform as well as he'd hoped to, thus starting our conversations at Counselling on Campus. It broke my heart to hear that I was one of the few people in his life who gave a damn about him, but he told me our talks always brightened his day.

When Ryder's men searched Matty's apartment, not only did they find the money Andrew stashed—which was around fifteen thousand dollars—they also found Andrew Robert's journals.

Matty could have lived off that money for another year or so. When I begged Denny to tell me about his living situation, he told me Matty had everything he needed but nothing more. The apartment was well kept. Matty didn't like dirty places and even though the place was cheap, it was tidy. He also said there was food in the fridge and clean clothes in his dresser which put me at ease.

Ryder brought me a photocopy of the journal as most of the stuff was then taken over by the police. It finally all fell together, just not for the reasons I thought. It didn't take me long to read it, but the answers were there.

The reasons I was stalked.

The reasons I was hated.

The reasons my family died.

The reasons I would be attacked.

Back in university, I had once comforted Andrew after he had an argument with his girlfriend. He had just paid her rent and then found out she was cheating on him. When Laura and I walked past the bench he was sitting on I set my hand on his shoulder and said, *"We're not all that bad, give it time and you'll find a good one. I promise."*

I was the first woman to give him hope.
Andrew worked with campus security doing technical stuff for them, thus giving him access to the security tapes where he watched my every move, becoming infatuated with me. When he put two and two together that I was the one who his brother was calling for help, he enlisted Matty in his plan to keep an eye on me. *For years*. Taking pictures to make sure the bad

men never came to hurt me. Andrew preyed on his innocent brother, tearing lives apart in the process.

It wasn't until I got pregnant with Lilly that he started to change. His infatuation turned to hate. Leading him to not only take my family from me, but to eventually end me as well. He wrote of suffering and pain, all of which I had caused him by not being the beautiful, kind woman he thought I had been.

There is no doubt in my mind Andrew had issues. Braumer's blood running through his veins ensured that. That's the most unfortunate part—Braumer. If it weren't for Andrew's obsession, none of this would have happened. Braumer was a sick fuck, yet had I not killed his son I wouldn't have ended up with him in the basement that night. But then I wouldn't have met Matty either.

This all started in a cold concrete room and it ended there.

Full circle.

Detective Miller and another male officer had questioned me in the hospital. I was fortunate enough to be let go, despite the fact that all the questions hadn't been answered. I'm not sure how Ryder or Miller pulled that all off. All I know is that due to my 'lack of memory' and lack of evidence regarding what happened in Andrew Robert's basement, I was free. Since there wasn't a soul who would push for a trial, and after everything that came out when Braumer attacked me in the basement (which I had to relive again while speaking to the officers), I was free to go.

Miller mentioned something regarding evidence at Braumer's that suggests he may have killed his own son, but I let it go. I know whatever it was wouldn't be true, and if it was planted, I have a good idea who put it there.

I want nothing to do with any of it, it's over and I need to move on.

"C'mon, beautiful."

Ryder's heady voice pulls me from the past and I follow him to the rear patio door. His house hasn't changed, not that I expected it to. The men from Callaghan Security stayed in Canada for a little over a week after Braumer attacked me. Ryder stayed the whole time. After I got out of the hospital, we didn't leave Jimmy's spare bedroom until it was time to go home.

Home.

I'd like to say I missed the cottage, and I missed North Carolina. I did in a way, but that's not what going home was; going home was being with Ryder and this just happens to be where we are most comfortable.

Strong arms wrap around my front and warm lips touch the top of my head. "She missed it here."

I nod my head in agreement as I watch Norma wade out into the cool water. The look of sheer happiness on my dog's face as the sun sets on the other side of the lake will forever be ingrained to my memory. "That she did," I reply.

I lean back against him, content and exhausted. Denny was kind enough to drive my BMW back from Canada along with my belongings. That left Ryder and I my other girl. My 1969 black Chevelle. With just an overnight bag in the trunk and Norma in the backseat, we made the trek home, arriving just in time to watch the sun go down.

"You hungry, beautiful?"

I open the door as Norma comes to it, "No. I just want to relax right now."

Grabbing my hand, Ryder leads me toward the stairs. It's a beautiful wooden staircase, open and airy just like the rest of his house. I watch briefly as Norma settles on the dog bed Ryder bought her before I follow him upstairs to the loft.

I could never see much from downstairs, but I had only been here twice. At the top of the staircase, I look to the right and notice a spare bedroom and a small bathroom. Between the two is an open area with a big window overlooking the water and a couple of comfy chairs. Ryder pulls me to the left into his bedroom.

"Wow Ry, this is stunning."

On the wall to the right is a king size bed, complete with slate-grey sheets and a cover dark enough it reminds me of his eyes. Holding my hand, he shows me the master bath which has a beautiful glass shower, complete with a bench and a rain-style shower head.

My favorite.

The walls are a soft grey color and the double vanity is black. To the left is a large tub, big enough for two, set underneath a window overlooking the water.

"I didn't take you as a decorator, but damn this is really nice, handsome. It still smells freshly painted."

He chuckles lightly and kisses my forehead. Placing his hands on either side of my face he says, "That's because it was finished while we were in Ontario."

I shake my head, not understanding. "You like bath's, beautiful. Can't say I'm much of a bath man but I got some old friends of mine that own a construction company to come and put a tub in and repaint. Up until last week it was just an empty space."

I look into his dark eyes. "No tub?"

He shakes his head. "No tub."

Confused, I ask, "but who doesn't have a tub?"

He grins at me. "I didn't. Now I do. For you."

Sometimes you meet people in life and wonder if they could get any kinder, any more thoughtful, any better than you already know them to be.

This moment proves the answer to be yes, you can. Because just when I think Ryder could not possibly top what he's already done, he has. Leaning up on my toes, I press my lips to his.

"Thank you. You didn't have to but thank you."

Deepening the kiss, he moves his hands down my back and under my rear. Knowing the drill, I wrap my legs around his back and allow him to carry me to bed. It's been a little over two weeks since we made love. Between my battered face, the constant headaches and my useless left arm, Ryder just held me every night. I've slept a lot these past few weeks, he has as well. While we haven't been intimate in every sense of the word, I know it's what we needed.

I needed to know he was there, and he needed to know that he could keep me. It felt good, letting that part of myself go. The part that hangs onto everything and controls every situation. It felt good to just be needed, and Ryder enjoyed being the one to provide that to me.

After he undresses me like he always does, revealing me like a present and cherishing me in every way, he puts us to bed. I snuggle into his side, and he pulls my chin up to press his lips to mine. "Sleep, beautiful."

Resting my head on his chest I listen to his heartbeat, grateful for the sound of it and content enough to close my eyes.

For the first time in years, I feel it.

I'm home.

Chapter Twenty-three

Ryder

I watch her as she slowly wakes. It's early, and she's not much of a morning person but we went to bed before dark and I know the smell of coffee will wake her even though the sun's not up yet. I watch her eyes flutter, waiting to see their beautiful, green intensity. The swelling is gone from her face, but she still has that light-yellow tinge from the bruising. Her stitches were taken out of her head before we left Ontario and I hate the two-inch mark on her flawless skin. I fight with myself constantly to not remember that day.

The day my woman was almost raped and killed.

The day I killed Detective Braumer.

As good as it felt, I wish I made him suffer more. The scar from her temple to her forehead fuels it. She's still the most beautiful woman in the world to me, but if I hate the reminder I have to wonder if she does too.

I don't talk about it, and neither does she. After that day in the shower at the hospital it was like we both silently agreed that that was where it would end. If she needs to talk, I'm here for her. I will be until the day I die. Until then, I keep my shit in check and do whatever I can to make her happy, and it pleases me to do so.

Not wanting to wait any longer, because I'm a pussy when it comes to her and I have no patience, I wrap the grey sheet around her body and lift her from the bed making sure to avoid hurting her arm. It still bothers her, so I take extra care and hold her close while I carry her out to the balcony at the end of my bed.

THE UGLY ROSES

The double doors are already open, letting in the cool morning breeze, but she won't mind. I watch her face as the dim light of dawn touches it. She opens her eyes and it hits me right in the heart, much like every other time. I'm the lucky bastard who she first lays her eyes on every day, and the light in her greens when she does so is something I will never forget.

I'm hers, and she's mine.

That's what reflects back and forth between us in that look, and the day that doesn't get my dick hard is the day you can call me a stupid son of a bitch.

"Morning, beautiful."

I watch the tip of her lips as she leans closer, pressing her lips to my neck. "Morning, handsome."

I feel her yawn against my skin, and I press my lips to her head, then her nose, then her mouth. She smiles back at me and I hope I never have to run my thumb across her forehead to smooth out her frowning when she sleeps.

I love my feisty woman; her stubbornness and sweetness complement each other. I love her sass, I love her wit and I love her attitude. But when I'm holding her in my arms, and her face is calm and content, her body relaxed and heartbeat even—she's fucking beautiful.

And she's mine.

"Oh my god," she says. Her eyes have left my face and she sees where we are. She was exhausted last night, and although I know she didn't miss the double patio doors off of my bedroom she definitely missed what she's looking at.

Her double-wide lounge with the giant, red cushion that matches my furniture on the lower deck is now up here. "I had Denny bring it over when he got back," I say to her.

I walk toward it and lay her down on what used to be her favorite thinking place. The place I watched her sit until the wee hours of the morning and the place she drank her coffee every day. I don't have the back up, but I put a few cushions on it as pillows. I already brought extra blankets outside before she woke up this morning as well, so she won't be cold.

The small table beside the lounge has two coffees sitting on it, but I don't bother handing one to her yet. They'll most likely be cold by the time we're done.

Fuck it, I'll make new ones.

Spreading her out below me, I grab the thick comforter I brought out and pull it over us as I settle myself between her legs. She brings both hands up to my face, careful with her right arm and gently brings her lips to mine.

"Thank you handsome, I'm feeling like an ass because you thought of everything and I've done nothing. You're making me look bad." She lets out a little laugh, semi-joking but I know she's serious. Elle does everything for everyone. She may come off as a cold-hearted bitch, but when she loves, she loves hard and does whatever she can for those closest to her.

"For starters, you could never look bad because you're the most beautiful woman I've ever met. Second, you love the fuck out of me, remember? So I'll forever be the one that's looking for ways to feel worthy of that."

Her eyes go soft and that's another thing I love about her. I'm not sure what happened since this last attack, and I do hope to fuck it's the last, but when I tell her she's beautiful I know she gets it.

THE UGLY ROSES

She finally fucking gets it.

I watch as her eyes get a little glossy before her sexy, raspy voice says, "I do love the fuck out of you, handsome," and following that statement she gives me the most breathtaking smile.

The one I'll never forget.

Not waiting any longer, I press my lips to hers, running my tongue along the seam of her lips asking for entrance. She gives it to me, and when the heat of her mouth hits mine I devour her. Soft, but aggressive enough that she will get everything I'm saying in the way my mouth moves with hers.

I grind against her, not able to prevent myself from doing so. I've been hard since I woke up and her naked body is underneath mine. She gasps, wanting it just as much as I do. "I need you, Ryder," she says between breaths that are few and far between.

"I need you too, Elle," I tell her as I move my mouth down her neck, across her collarbone before pulling one of her pert nipples into my mouth. I circle my tongue around it before moving my hand down the side of her toned body. When I reach the back of her leg I pull it up so she can hook it around my back.

I smooth my hands up the back of her thigh and over her luscious ass before they find her wet center.
"Please don't tease me this time, Ryder."

I chuckle around her tit, I'm not teasing her. I'm making sure she's ready. I was a little worried these past few weeks, not just how she would react after almost being raped but also worried how I would. I've never been here before, and I wasn't sure how to navigate through something like this.

We soon found our rhythm though, and it seemed we both just wanted to be there, for each other. We found our solace together after that nightmare, and I have no intention of teasing her or making her wait.

I can do that later.

"Wouldn't dream of it, beautiful. Not this time."

She sighs when I pull my fingers out from between her legs and being the selfish bastard I am I pull my lips from her nipple in favor of putting my fingers in my mouth. I love all of her. Her smells, and definitely her taste. I watch her pupils dilate as she watches me. I know she loves watching me taste her; she just needs to know I love it more.

Her hands move down my back, and she uses her right arm, the good one to pull me forward. Releasing my fingers from my mouth I hold her head in my hands and press my lips to hers before pushing inside.

"I love you, beautiful," I whisper against her lips. She wraps her legs around my body, and I push in to the root, watching her eyelids flutter in pleasure.

"I love you too, Ryder," she says, followed by the moan that I love.

I roll my hips into hers, and she pushes back against them. It's not fast, it's not slow. It's what Elle calls my *punishing pace*, which brings her to orgasm.

Every. Single. Time.

I move my arm under her back, pulling her closer to me if that's at all possible. All I know is that I need to devour her. Make us one, in every form of the word. The warmth of our bodies is a stark contrast to the cooler morning as I worship this woman underneath me. I hope to convey that through every movement of my body.

Every touch.

Every kiss.

"You're close," I tell her, because I know her body better than I know my own. I know every sensitive spot. Every freckle, every scar. I know all of her and yet I want to know more.

I want everything.

"Keep your eyes open, beautiful. You know I need your eyes," I plead with her. She nods, too far gone for words but I watch as the green of her eyes turns brighter, and the light sheen of unshed tears threatens to run down her cheeks.

"I love you so much, so fucking beautiful."

She clamps her internal muscles down on my cock and I watch as her mouth opens, fighting for air, unable to stop sounds of pleasure from deep in her throat. "Agghhh, fuck!" She barely gets the curse out of her mouth before I swallow it with my own.

I roll my hips, once, twice, three times before burying myself to the hilt, emptying everything I have inside in her, unable to stop the growl from my mouth. The nails of her right hand still dig deep into my back and her body shivers and shudders underneath mine as her orgasm runs long throughout her body.

I press my damp forehead to hers, not bothering to pull out because she's warm and I know she likes me there. Her smooth hands run through my hair and around my jaw, holding my mouth to hers as she whispers, "home." It was said so softly, if I wasn't this close, I wouldn't have heard her.

I pull away so I can see her eyes, hoping she'll explain. Elle a few months ago wouldn't, but the beautiful woman underneath me today continues to surprise me.

"I didn't know, or maybe I forgot what it felt like, but it's home," she says.

I watch the dark clouds that have forever been over her head part. I watch the clarity set into her beautiful green eyes, but I'm still confused so I ask her, "what's home, beautiful?"

She smiles that sexy as fuck smile she graced me with this morning. It brings out a small dimple in her cheek that I never knew she had and makes her look like the most carefree woman in the world. One I've never met until today but plan to hold onto for the rest of my life.

"I didn't know it before, I just thought I needed to leave Ontario and I needed to be here, because it was my calm place. I figured it out though, I didn't need this beach, and I didn't need North Carolina. I love it but I didn't *need* it." Her eyes get serious and she holds my face in her hands. "I just needed you, and North Carolina just happens to be where you are. *You're* home, Ryder. I haven't felt home in a long time, but you're it. You're my home. So, thank you for that."

For the first time in my life I'm at a loss for words, I don't like words much—I like action. I also haven't felt this lump in my throat or the irregular beat in my chest since I was told my mother was dying of cancer.

I'm her home.

I let out a small gasp, fighting for air into my lungs because my life just told me something that means more to me than any 'I love you' ever would. I remember her words in the hospital, in the shower; this is what she meant.

This is what she wanted to give me.

I fight the blurriness in my eyes, feeling like a pussy while at the same moment knowing I'm the luckiest prick on the planet. I watch the smile on her face reappear as she notices what's going through my head, watching the emotions play out on my face. I give her everything and hiding who I am is not something I would keep from her.

Fighting for air, and struggling to speak I manage to say, "You remember in the hospital, when you told me 'I love you' didn't seem like enough? So, you told me you loved the fuck out of me and that would have to do?"

I watch the recognition of our conversation play out over her beautiful face as she nods, "yes, I remember."

I press my forehead to hers, holding onto her pretty little stubborn head. "You didn't just give me enough, beautiful. You gave me everything. And that's the best feeling in the whole fucking world, and no *I love you* would ever top that."

I devour her mouth, reaching over to the bottom shelf on the table. I was going to wait, not because I wanted to but because I'm still a fucking sucker for this woman and I wanted to make it perfect. Perfect isn't us, but this moment is the best one of my life so I don't see the reason to wait any longer.

Leaning to her right side, I take some of the weight off her body and watch her fractured arm settle across my chest. The fact that I'm still buried inside her and half-hard only completes the moment.

Lightly taking her hand, I look into her sated eyes. "I'm probably going to fuck something up. At some point it's inevitable. I hope I don't, but if I told you life will be perfect from here on out it would make me a liar."

She smirks, tears still lingering in her eyes. "I'm the moodiest, handsome, and this life of ours isn't a fairytale."

I love that as serious as she could be she's able to lighten the situation. Life is not perfect, she knows that above anyone. We've both been through shit and are smart enough and old enough to know that sometimes life hands you an ugly fucking curveball and if you're strong enough, you'll be able to hit that. Might not make a home run, but you'll work through the bases and have the backs of those around of you.

"I'm a moody prick too, and you're stubborn as hell so I guess we'll complement one another in the oddest of ways. Regardless, you're still the only woman in the world I want to spend the rest of my life with."

I watch her eyes go from sated to shocked as I carefully slip the ring on her finger. I know how she feels about family, marriage and love. A lot I learned from her, but I also listened to Jimmy. Not wanting her to feel pressured, I look into her eyes and say, "I don't ever expect you to put a white dress on. I don't expect you to give me children or have dinner on the table every night. I don't expect anything from you, except that you love me, and I remain your home.

"I'm a selfish prick so I'd be lying if I said I didn't want my last name to be yours, but if that's not up for negotiation then I will never push you. I just want you, Elle. I want to keep you and if you'd do me the honor of wearing that ring, even without the dress, the last name and the kids, you'd make me the luckiest man in the world. I just want you. It's as simple as that."

I watch the tears run down her beautiful face, she never looked at the ring but that's not her, she doesn't care. This moment is bigger than the jewelry and I respect the fuck out of her for being that way.

"Say something, beautiful," I whisper against her lips.

She presses hers back to mine, eager and hard, and I taste the saltiness of her tears. She pushes lightly against my chest with her left hand, gasping when she finally gets a look at the ring before she moves her eyes to mine.

"I didn't need the ring," she chokes out between breathes. "I just needed you. Shit, I never thought I would be here Ryder, I didn't," she sobs. "But now that I am, I don't want to be anywhere else. Nothing would make me happier, Ryder. I'll take your name with pleasure, and if you truly want the dress, I think I could throw that in too," she giggles.

Fucking giggles.

Other than when she's talking dirty to me, I've never heard a more beautiful sound.

Jayne Elle Callaghan.

I'm keeping her.

Chapter Twenty-four

Elle

I can't help but look at my left hand as I pull the car door open. The ring Ryder got me a few months ago still takes my breath away but I'm not about flash. He knows that. He also put a lot of thought into what he gave me, and I am more thankful for his thoughtfulness than I am for the ring.

Apparently one of his first jobs with Callaghan Security was for a popular jeweler, not Tiffany and Co., but a jeweler that was known for incredibly unique handmade creations. Long story short he and his team discovered who the thieving CEO was, and he also made a friend.

Ryder worked with Phillip DeSanto to create what can only be described as beautiful. The ring is an inch wide on the top. Multiple vines wrap underneath the cherry blossom which somehow blooms into a floating water lily, if that makes any sense. It combines my past with my future, and in the center of the platinum creation is what can only be described as Ryder's eyes, joined into one. A giant, black diamond lays among my memories, and the inscription cut inside the vines is what makes it us: *Keep me, 'cause I sure as fuck am not letting you go.*

Many women would cringe at the crass word on their wedding ring. Good thing I'm not most woman and while I may be kinder and friendlier, I still don't give two fucks what someone else thinks of me.

I've gone through my misery, grief and hardships. I've went through my stubborn bitch faze where I hated the world. I've been knocked down a time or two only to drag myself back up. But now I have Ryder to put me back together and it's the most beautiful thing in the world.

THE UGLY ROSES

I love that man with everything I have, and I show him daily. I haven't put the white dress on, but life has been perfect and despite my general moodiness, it's complete. I still have worrisome things I need to speak to him about, but I don't dwell on it as I open the door to my Chevelle.

"Where are we now, Gina?" Matty asks in excitement. I've never forgotten about him, nor have I left him behind.

It took about a month before we could get him to North Carolina. I had to heal and so did he. We also had Cabe working around the clock to get him American Citizenship and into his house. I'm not sure how he pulled it off so fast, but I assume Callaghan Security has connections in high places, so I didn't bother to ask. Willow Beach welcomed Matty with open arms. I'm grateful that Ryder was with me when we picked Matty up from the airport to escort him to his new home because I was an emotional mess.

As we expected, he loved it. Willow Beach is a mixture of individuals from many walks of life, but mainly older, developmentally challenged adults who just need a small hand here and there, and a kind group of people who understand them better.

I would have loved to move Matty next door to me, but after many conversations with Ryder, and professionals who work with individuals like Matty on regular basis, this is where he would be happiest. After many sleepless nights and phone calls, I put my own selfish wants to keep him close aside and bought him a house at Willow Beach.

After meeting some of the staff as well as other residents, I knew this was where he would be happy and that's what's important. Matty is a part of me and I will forever be mother hen with him after what we went through together, but after watching him interact with the people there, playing ring toss and having a community barbecue, I knew this was his place.

He had a home.

I'd like to say I embraced my inner bitch and dragged him to my home where I could keep him safe, away from someone who might speak to him unfairly, but I didn't.

I couldn't.

He was just too happy.

So now, after getting him settled at the Willow Beach community yesterday, Ryder and I have taken him to his new job. It's only a mile up the road and he can ride the bike we bought him here. If it's cold, he can use the bus.

I grab Matty's hand, ignoring his question of where we are as Ryder walks behind us. I didn't park out front; I pulled into the side of the building so he didn't see the sign. I pull open the side door used for employees and walk Matty into the building.

"There's a dog!" Matty exclaims as he drops my hand and heads for the Labrador. I let him coddle for a few moments before Nancy comes around the corner, excited to meet her new worker.

"Well hello there," she says, bright smile on her friendly face. "I heard you're a hard worker and might be able to help me out around here."

Matty stands up from petting the sweet dog and has a confused look on his face, switching from staring at Ryder and I to staring at Nancy. "My friends brought me here," he says uncomfortably. I don't mean to make him uncomfortable, so I clear the confusion.

"You wanted to work with animals Matty, and this is an animal clinic. Nancy needs help with animals, not only to look after them but to help her out around the clinic. I told her I knew someone perfect for the job and I was hoping that you'd like to take it, but it's entirely up to you."

If I was a stronger woman, the woman I was months ago, I'd be able to stop the tears from gathering in my eyes. But I can't.

"I can help? Here?" He questions before turning very serious, "Miss Marion said I was a good helper and I went to school to work with animals, Nancy, so I'd like to help!" Matty exclaims.

The wetness runs down my cheeks. I don't make a move to stop them as Ryder wraps his arms around me from behind. I look to Nancy noticing she's about as choked up as I am. She's clearly a good person and sensitive not just with animals, but kind people as well.

Clearing her throat, she says, "Matty, I would love it if you could help. It would mean a lot to me and the animals. I have a baby Jack Russel in the back that needs fed and attention around the clock. I don't have the time, and sometimes you'd need to take the animal home with you, but if you can make the time it would be a big help."

I catch the sob before it escapes my throat, and remind myself once again when I leave here I will thank my angels in heaven for putting kind people in my new friend's life.

"I can do it, Nancy! I love animals! Miss Marion let me help a baby robin bird when its mom died, and it lived, Nancy! I saved it!"

I turn my head into Ryder's chest, thankful that he knows I can't keep my shit together when I witness kind things such as this. I never cried before, ever. Now when I see something sweet and vulnerable it takes all I have to leave the house without a box of fucking Kleenex.

"Well, let's do a walk through, Matty. I have a lot of things that need doing, and you and I are going to be busy. You up for it?" Nancy asks.

Matty smiles a big one that melts my entire heart. He marches the few steps toward me and puts his arms around Ryder and me. "Thanks, friends! Thanks so much!" Turning around he announces, "I'm ready, Nancy! Gina showed me the bus schedule and I can stay until just after supper time!"

I don't bother reminding him that he has a bike at home or telling him we stocked his fridge. He already knows, and Nancy has worked with people from Willow Beach before so she's familiar with the ropes.

Ryder pulls me toward the exit. As much as I'm not ready to leave, I know he's telling me it's time. Time to the let the bird fly the coop, time to let Matty have responsibility in doing what he always wanted to do.

I follow him, not thinking about the fact that I now own *Second Chance*, the animal rescue center that was crumbling until Cabe informed me and I bought it.
Whatever makes Matty happy, whatever makes him whole.

I'll make it happen.

***

I walk beside Ryder, tears streaming down my once miserable face as he leads me to the Chevelle. Matty loves this car, and since we only live thirty minutes away, I couldn't *not* pick him up in it.

"You gonna be okay, beautiful?"

Ryder has twisted me around, so my back is leaning against the car, his face close to mine. I'm not ready to talk about it in depth yet, because I don't think I can talk without crying. I nod my head and simply say, "I'm okay, let's go home before I ball my face off like a needy woman and I make an ass of myself." I chuckle.

It's not lost on Ryder that my humor is masking what's underneath, but I'm thankful that being as we are in a semi-public space, he grants my wishes and drives us home.

Chapter Twenty-five

One week later.

No.

It can't be.

Not fucking possible.

To say I'm shocked to shit would be a huge understatement. I don't know what to do, I don't know who to talk to and I have no idea where the fuck I'm going or what I'm doing. What started as a normal day taking Ryder and his men lunch at Callaghan Security before they left on a job for the week has quickly gone to shit.

My world just turned upside down.

I feel sick, I feel lost, and all I know is I need to get out of here. I need space. I need to think and tie up loose ends.

Pulling into the drive at Ryder's house—*our house*—I do the one thing I've been good at. The one thing that makes me have purpose and allows me to get my head on straight. Quickly packing a small suitcase, and getting Norma in the car, I run.

Running.

It's what I do best.

Do I want to leave?
No.

But I have to.

THE UGLY ROSES

It's what Jayne O'Connor would do, it's what Harley Green would have done and it's what Elle Davidson perfected.

So I run.

***

I have trouble breathing as I drive, like a bag of stones is hanging around my neck, pulling me toward the ground. The memories of my past keep playing over and over in my mind and I don't know whether I want to cry or hit something. I breathe deep through my nose, and out through my mouth. Over and over for miles.

How the fuck did this happen?

The past few months with Ryder have been bliss. Everyone has ups, downs, fuck ups. I don't expect life to be a fairytale and I am living proof that those are a crock of shit. No life is perfect, but this past little while mine has come incredibly close to being so.

After all that I've been through, after everything I've overcome, I finally found a little peace. My mind has calmed, the nightmares are few and far between and when they happen, I have Ryder to comfort me. Why couldn't I have stayed in that bubble? Why does this cruel thing we call life have to throw another fork in the road and make me second guess what I have been dead set against for years?

The vibrating of my phone on the dash of my Chevelle snaps me to the present, I know I can't ignore him, and I would never want to. Ryder deserves all that is good in the world and I don't want to worry while he's away on a job.

I clear my throat. "Hey, handsome."
"Where are you, beautiful?"

Not wanting to lie but giving him little, I say, "just out for a drive."

The other end of the phone is silent, I wonder if he's onto me and he confirms. "Elle, our job got pushed back. Want to tell me why I just walked in the door to our house and one of your bags is gone, along with all that girl shit you leave out on the vanity in the bathroom?"

I gasp. I wasn't expecting him to be home for six days.

Six days for me to find answers, give explanations and sort my head.

"Ryder, I…"

He cuts me off. "Don't lie to me, beautiful. I love you, please don't fucking lie to me."

"I never lie to you; how could you say that?" I'm shocked he would imply such a thing, especially after what we've been through this past year and how much we've overcome.

He grunts. "Omitting information could be the same thing, Elle. Where are you?"

"Don't push me, Ryder," I say low and determined. I know running is not always the best idea, but it's how I deal with things and I can't change that right now. I choke back the tears wanting to escape. My emotions are all over the place but of course I embrace the only one that gives me power, the one that keeps me, well, me.

Anger.

"I have laid myself bare for you, Ryder Callaghan. You know more about me than any other person on the fucking planet."

He sighs. "I know you have. But I'll ask again, where are you?"

I ignore his question. "I need a few days, Ryder. I love you."

"Dammit Elle, tell me what the hell happened between fucking you on the desk in my office and now? Because when I last saw you there was a smile on your face and now you're scaring the shit out of me!"

I push the wonderful memory of our nooner in his office out of my mind and try to placate him. "It may be hard for you to understand, but sometimes I need time. This is that time, Ryder. I love you, I truly do. But I need to be alone for a few days."

"Jesus Elle, I thought you were past this shit!" he growls into the phone. "I love you, come back home and we'll sort whatever the hell it is you think you need to sort on your own."

"I don't need you to sort it, Ryder! I'm a grown woman if you didn't already clue into that fact."

He snarls, clearly pissed off. "A grown woman who is currently acting like goddamn child! Shit gets tough and you run, but what you don't realize is that you're running in the wrong fucking direction!"

"Fuck you, Ryder. Don't you dare judge me for running. If I remember correctly, running saved my life, proven by the fact that I'm arguing with you on the phone right now when all I wanted was to clear my head. I love you, Ryder. I'll be home soon. Goodbye."

I power the phone off when I'm done, not wanting to argue anymore, not wanting him to follow me. There are things I need to do, people I need to thank and hopefully when that shit's done I'll have that clear fucking conscience everyone talks about, but I've never understood.

I need space to figure this out.

Because for the first time in a long time, I'm completely fucking lost.

Chapter Twenty-six

I leave the door to my motel room open as I wait for Norm to finish her business. I'm happy to say the majority of my paranoia is gone but living a life of looking over my back for over a year means that some habits are hard to let go of.

I toss my suitcase on the bed and shut the door behind Norm. It's late, or early. Four in the morning to be exact. I don't plan on staying here long, just a day or two before I move on to my next destination.

I take a long, hot shower, washing off the road grime and climb into bed. I already hate it. The mattress is hard and Ryder's not here. I don't want to be harsh with him, but the way he spoke to me on the phone was uncalled for. If he had went on his business trip, he would have been none the wiser of my whereabouts.

His coming home put a damper on my plan but I'm still going to see it through.

***

I turn my phone on as Norma and I walk down the sidewalk. It's a mild evening and since the motel was close there's no reason to drive. Plus, Norma doesn't need to be cooped up in the car any longer than necessary.

It takes a few moments for the beeps and buzzes to finish before I can actually see my home screen. Some days I miss my shitty old burner phones. I temporarily ignore the text from Ryder and open up one from Matty. He knows my new number (for a regular smart phone). He also learned to text.

I respond to every one of them.

It melts my heart when I see a photo of him, holding onto a baby kitten, bottle feeding it. The warmth and happiness reflecting in his eyes melts my heart. He is truly the sweetest human being I have ever met. Not wanting to waste any more time I press connect.

"Gina!"

I smile at the sound of his sweet voice. "Hey pal, how's your day going?"

He laughs. "It's really good, Gina. Did you get my picture?"

I nod, a little choked for words but realizing he can't see me. "I did get it, Matty. It looks like you're doing a really good job at Second Chance."

"I am, Gina! Nancy took that picture for me, I told her I wanted to show my friends how good of a helper I am."

I sigh, content that he's so happy, absorbing his words. "That's great, I'm happy for you."

"I'm happy too, you know why?" He doesn't give me the chance to answer. "Because I got to bring a kitten home! Someone found it on the side of the road and it still needs its mom, so Nancy said it would have a better chance if I took her home and fed her with the bottle every few hours! Isn't that awesome, Gina?"

"It sure is, buddy." I'm choked up.
"I can do it, Gina! I set my alarm and everything. Every four hours I have to feed her!"

"I know you can do it buddy and I'm very proud of you."

He's quiet, and I know it's because like usual when anyone gives him praise, he takes a moment to let it sink in before he speaks with a little more hope in his voice. "Thanks, friend. I have to go now Gina because Terry asked me if I wanted to bring the kitten to movie night."

Terry is one of the other residents I met at Willow Beach, and I'm happy to hear Matty is interacting with other people, joining them at the community house for movie night. "It's okay, Matty. I'll talk to you soon, okay?"

"Okay, Gina!"

He hangs up before I can say goodbye, or I love you. But that's okay, because he's happy.

Chapter Twenty-seven

I open the door and allow Norma to walk in ahead of me. I forgot tonight was women's self-defense night. I remember the last time I was in the same room with some of these women—I couldn't stand a single fucking one of them.

There are a few who are no bother, some shy women I definitely have more respect for as opposed to the others, like the one with a fully painted face, tits falling out of her sports bra, hand on Brocks arm as she asks him a question.

I clear my throat before saying loudly, "he's married sweetheart, and if you want to keep that hand of yours, I suggest you remove it."

Both Brock and the slutty chick whip their heads around. Her face holds a tight scowl. I want to tell her it makes her look like a wrinkly-faced pug, but I refrain and focus on Brock, who has a giant smile on his sexy face.

Pulling away from the hooker, Brock strides toward me. We've only ever hugged twice but when I see him coming, I reach my arms up and allow him to pick me off the ground with his big, beefy arms.

"Holy fuck, didn't think I'd see ya again, babe." Following the comment, he puts me down on my feet and puts his hands on my shoulders. "Is everything alright?"

His face is full of concern. It doesn't need to be. "I'm good, Brock. Really, I'm good." I give him more of a smile than he's ever seen, it's not huge but it's something. Seeming placated he nods his head.
"Vinny, takeover would ya?"

I watch Vinny come out of the office, taking over the class. He's not as good looking, but the women don't seem to mind.

"How've you been?" He motions to the far wall, away from prying ears and we both move in that direction to take a seat. "Norm hasn't gotten any smaller, I see."

I chuckle. "No, she still eats well. Hope you don't mind her in here."

He takes a seat and looks over at me. "If I said she wasn't would you kick her out?"

I shake my head. "Probably not," I reply with a smirk. "Well, how have you been Brock West, it's been a while." I don't want to do the idle crap talk but I'm working my way up to something and I know he'll humor me until I get there.

"I've been good, really good. Gym's doing great, Sam's bakery is doing better, and we just bought a new house," he says with true bliss in his eyes.

"I'm happy for you. That's good, Brock." I clear my throat. "I came here for a reason actually." I ignore his eyes, feeling nervous is not something I like, nor is it something I'm familiar with.

He puts his hand on mine, stilling it until I make eye contact. "You know you'll get no pressure from me, just support. Whatever it is, just say it."

I kind of missed him. I don't miss a lot of people, but Brock is just something different, he's a lot like Denny actually; they both have this thing about them that just makes you want to hang onto them forever because they're so easy going.

"I lied to you." He looks confused. "A lot. I lied to you a lot, but I can assure you it was for a good fucking reason."

Shaking his head, he says, "You're here, you look good. Whatever babe, back burner it if you need to. It looks like it's stressin' you out to have to tell me."

I give him a little smile. "I have to tell you, Brock. I'm trying to get one of those things people talk about. You know, a clear conscience? A clean slate, no baggage? I'm not too familiar with it but I'm trying."

He laughs. "Whatever you need to do, babe."

Leaning back against the wall, I dive in. "My real name is Jayne Elle O'Connor and I'm from Ontario." He's shocked for a small moment before he too leans back against the wall, sensing there is more where that came from. "Long story short, because Brock, it is a long fucking story, I was running." I take a deep breath. "A few years ago, my mother, father and daughter were killed in a car accident. I didn't know it at the time, but it was murder. A while after that I was kidnapped and tortured for three days, and my daughter's father was also killed during that time.

"It's been over a year since that all happened. I came here so I could tell you if it weren't for your help, if you hadn't taught me what I know, taught me how to fight back, well I don't think I'd be sitting here with you right now."

I swallow and chance a look at him. His face is pale, completely lost for words. Not being a pussy and giving him the respect he deserves I look him in the eye when I say the rest. "I was put in jail a few months ago, and while a guard was on the verge of raping me along with another male a few weeks later; it was your words that kept me alive." I blink, letting a single tear roll down my cheek as I say the words he once said to me, *"Never stay down, Elle. You get back up, you keep fucking going. The longer you're down, the better chance he has at keeping you there. Don't give him that chance, Elle. You fight, until you can't stand anymore. When that's done, you fucking fight some more. And when it's done you run, run as fast as you fucking can."*

I give him a small smile. "You may not know it, but I'm pretty certain you saved my life, Brock. So, I came here to say thank you."

I watch his hands that balled into fists midway through the conversation unclench as he brings his hands to shocked, misty eyes. "Fuck babe," he chokes out, clearly emotional from my words.

Putting my hand on his shoulder, I pull him forward and place a kiss on his cheek. "Thank you."

Strong arms wrap around me. I let him hold me as long as he needs to. You never know what kind of people he meets while coaching his self-defense classes, but I needed to tell him this so that one day if he ever thinks he hasn't made an impact, hasn't helped, he'll remember this moment and know just how much what he taught me means.

It means everything.

Pulling away, he assesses me with new eyes. I just gave him a bit of a new person he knew nothing about.

"The marks on your wrists, your neck. Fuck, Elle. I just...fuck!" Standing up, he paces in front of me. I know it's a lot to take in. I've lived it. Brock is also a caring and compassionate man so he truly feels what I just told him.

Moving to stand in front of him, I place a hand on his shoulder. "I'm okay now, Brock. It's been a long time coming, but I'm okay."

Shaking his head he says, "Jesus, I don't know what to say, Elle. I just don't have words."

I give him a squeeze. "They're overrated anyway, and you know I'm not much of a talker."

He laughs a little, knowing too well that no truer words have been spoken.

His eyes turn stormy. "What now? Is the guy in prison? Dead?"

I shake my head sadly at him. "My part of talking about it is over, I'm sure if you Google my name you'll understand more, but keep in mind not everything you read is true."

He nods sadly, not because I'm not telling him more but because he probably has that whole information overload thing going on.

"Will you meet me at Sam's bakery in the morning? I have a favor to ask of you," I say.

With a quick chin jerk, he replies, "anything."

"Meet you there at eight," I tell him, giving him one last small smile, watching his face fall the minute I turn around. It might have been smarter to tell him this stuff in the morning, but I wasn't thinking things through and shit changes quickly. Now it's out there. I just hope when he goes to bed tonight, he doesn't dwell on the bad and instead feels more content with the fact he saved a life, even if it was indirectly.

Chapter Twenty-eight

"I'm proud of you, Elle. I'm sure you've heard that a lot, but you're a damn strong woman and I'm proud of you."

I give Brock a look of confusion, knowing he probably Googled me last night but not sure what he's talking about.

"I called Denny. He filled in some blanks for me. I wasn't trying to pry into your life, but..." He leaves it hanging there. I'm not upset he called Denny, but I only came here to tell him thank you, tell him why, and of course leave out the rest of my dreaded past that I don't need to speak of ever again.

Leaning up I give him a kiss on the cheek. "Take care of my girl, alright? I'll be back in a day or two to pick her up," I tell him as I hug him goodbye. It was great to eat some of Sam's delicacies this morning and catch up, not that there was a lot to catch up on because I never spoke much, but Sam's a bit of a rambler so she filled the void between chatting with other customers. I'm grateful he waited until now to bring up his knowledge of my past because I don't think it's something Sam needed to know.

Denny steps back and dangles the keys to my Chevelle. "Trust me babe, I wouldn't hurt her."

I smile at him and walk across the tarmac to the small plane. One of the perks to being a free woman is that my money is no longer tied up in Canada. I have no use for the majority of it, mostly because I didn't do a damn thing to earn the eight million dollars I inherited when my parents were killed. Also, because I don't live a lavish lifestyle and I never intend to. My parents, Gary and Susan were incredibly humble people and I intend to follow in their footsteps.

I've never spent this much money on something so mundane, but like fuck if I was going to put Norma in a cage and have her stored underneath the main cabin on a commercial flight. I also didn't feel like making a sixteen-hour drive with her in the car after just making an eleven-hour trip to Indianapolis.

I wave over my shoulder as I board the private plane. It's beautiful. It also cost a small fortune but it's worth it and my dog will be comfortable. Brock waits until the cabin door is closed and we're heading down the runway before he climbs into my car. He's a good friend and a great person. I look out into the clouds and say a small thank you and a prayer to my family for bringing such an amazing person into my life.

***

"Thank you for flying with us, Ms. O'Connor."

I shake the pilot's hand. "It's Elle and thank you for being so accommodating on such short notice."

He tips his hat to me and I head to the waiting SUV just off the runway. I didn't figure a taxi would like me putting my big, hairy girl in the backseat, so I called a car service and requested an SUV. I could have rented my own car, but I was informed there is no car rental office at the tiny private airport. So, either way I would have had to get Norma and I from A to B.

"Good afternoon, I'm Ted. I'll be your driver today."
I reach out and shake his hand. "Nice to meet you, Ted."

He takes my small luggage and I move ahead of him to open up the rear hatch for Norma. She's familiar with the process of getting in and out of vehicles, so like a good girl she jumps right in and I hop in the back seat.

"Where to, Miss?"

THE UGLY ROSES

Thankful he didn't call me ma'am, I tell him the area I'm
heading to and we pull out on the highway. The drive is quiet,
and even though I just had time to myself on the plane, I enjoy
the silence. I watch the somewhat familiar scenery pass by
before I tell him our destination is just ahead on the right-hand
side. Putting the blinker on, slowing down he asks, "you sure
about that?" Eyeing the dozens of bikes parked out front of
Blacktop, I nod my head. "Yes, I'm sure."

He gives me no answer, but dutifully pulls in the lot. I put
my hand between the seats and hand him a very good tip.
"Thank you, Ted. I'll get my bag."

He looks down at the wad of cash, a little shocked by the
amount I placed there. But he looks like a kind soul and
probably has better shit to do than drive all day. "Thank you,
Miss. Thank you very much"

I give him a small smile and gather up my bag and my dog.
When the SUV pulls out of sight there are already three bikers
standing out on the front step of Blacktop. One smiles and
crouches down on his haunches. "Norma! How's my favorite
girl doin'?"

Norm wags her tail and smiles that sweet dog smile before
waddling over to Digger. I may have spent a few weeks here
about a year ago, but I didn't make a lot of friends. The men
were good to me, but I by no means shot the shit with many.
Norma on the other hand, was welcomed with open arms and I
never had to worry about her here. The guys took good care of
her and she was fed well.

"That's my girl, ya missed me?" Digger asks, holding my
hefty dog close to his body. As usual, Norm soaks up the
attention as I walk up the steps.

"Hey, fellas."

Digger nods. "Good to see ya, darlin'. Tiny's inside."

197

"Thanks," I say, giving the other two men I don't really know a nod before heading inside.

Sometimes change is good, sometimes it's terrible. Being as this was one of the first places I felt safe after Andrew and my three days of hell, I'm happy it hasn't changed one bit.

The floors are still sticky, and it smells like hookers and cigarettes, with a stale beer or two. I look to the left, for his regular table and spot Tiny at the head of it. Five others surround him, all hanging on every word he says.

Respect.

The conversation is important, because there are no scantily clad women running around the place, and other than the table of five and a few other bikers at the bar, the place is empty. I don't bother disturbing him, he gave all his time and attention to me once and I'm not in a rush this time.

I close my eyes and breathe for a moment. It's not the cleanest air being as it smells so strongly of smoke. It makes me crave one, but I think better of it. I'm saved from thinking about it when a booming warm voice says, "I 'aint got much time left in this shithole. You keep standin' there girl, I might be dead before ya get the chance to say hello."

I smile before opening my eyes, grateful regardless of his ancient status, he still hasn't lost the wit and wisdom I love so much. Glancing toward him, I take in his kind old eyes and long, grey hair he still keeps tied at the back of his neck. His eyes hold a history—a very long one. I'm proud to know this wonderful man and I push off the wall to tell him so.

"This shithole isn't ready to let you go yet," I say smirking, a double meaning to my words. I know he gets it. Swallowing, he waves his hand in a shooing motion to the other gentlemen around the table. "Back to work, ya lazy bastards. Rather stare at my girl than any 'a your ugly mugs." The men stand. I give a slight shake of my head at Tiny's antics. Remy and Keg give me a head to toe perusal, and a shit eatin' grin. In the past they never outright checked me out, but my spine wasn't as straight then and I kept my broken body well covered in layers of clothing.

Today I'm in a loose, black tank top with wide straps and skinny jeans with my black boots. I still wear my wrist cuffs, but my neck is no longer covered. I raise my eyebrow in question and Remy just shakes his head before heading off. Tiny doesn't like to be kept waiting so I brush them aside and lean down, kissing the old man's cheek. "How are you old man?"

He does his own perusal, but not like his men. Tiny's perusal is solely on my eyes and I have no doubt he can see everything behind them. "I'm good girl, real good. So are you."

His smile is contagious. I return it with a big one of my own. "Yes, Tiny. I'm doing well."
He nods and says, "I know, wasn't a question."

I can't help but shake my head at him, of course he knows. When you've lived as long as he has you know just about everything.

"Ya didn't just come to say hello either," he says, taking a sip of the beer in front of him.

I sigh. "No, I also came to say a few things and tell you who I am."

"Already know who ya are girl, don't need to tell me."

I tilt my head to the side, wondering how he knows. "What's my name, old man?"

He shuffles, slightly uncomfortable. "Good lad comes around here sometimes, good friends with Remy. Also good friend 'a yours from what I hear, 'cause he sat down and had a beer with me last month and told me so. Also told me thank you, for helpin' you out." I lean back in my chair knowing it was Jimmy and he leans forward. "Told him I didn't know what he was talkin' about and he told me all about a woman named Jayne."

Looking up from his beer, his eyes find mine again. "Glad you're doin' good, girl. Had I have known what you was runnin' from, I'd 'a kept you right here. I'd 'a kept you safe."

Sincerity and guilt shines through his eyes and I don't for one second want him to feel that way. "You did exactly what I asked of you and then some, Tiny. I survived a long time as Elle Davidson and without you that wouldn't have been possible."

Deep in thought he replies, "yes, you did *survive*. But ya didn't *live*."
I nod in agreement. "You're right, I didn't."

Warm ancient hands engulf my left one. He looks at the ring then back to my face. "But you are now, and so long as you keep doin' that you'll make this old man happy. Everybody needs to live girl, life ain't just about survivin' 'cause ya ain't got a life until you live. Happy to see you figured that out."

Swallowing past the lump in my throat and ignoring the tightness in my chest I tell him, "thank you, Tiny."

Ever the modest one he says, "ain't nothin' to thank me for. You bein' well is all the thanks I need."

Ignoring me in favor of Norma as she rests her head on his lap, I take one last deep breath and let it go. I've been a lot of things in my life, but a liar is not one of them, that was until I needed to lie in order to save my life.

It's over.

My conscience is cleared.

Now to get the rest of me in order.

Chapter Twenty-nine

I crawl out of the clean sheets, mighty impressed with how quick Tiny can pulls things off. Although I shouldn't be surprised. After I announced that I wasn't leaving until the next day, Tiny had a couple of prospects clean a room upstairs for me. I couldn't fight the laugh when he hollered, *"prospects! Clean out a room. Clean sheets, clean floors and do the bathroom while you're at it! If ya can't lick the toilet seat when you're done, I'll be starin' at you're backs when I kick your asses out the door."*

Of course, like the dutiful young prospects they are, they did as they were told. When I stayed here before I kept a bottle of Lysol handy at all times and I'm happy that it wasn't needed this time around.

After a much-needed trip to the bathroom and a quick clean up, I change my clothes and grab my bag. It will probably be the last time I see this place. I said what I needed to, and even though my head is not completely sorted, I feel lighter.

I power up my phone as I walk down the hallway, as usual I check Matty's text first and send him a quick text back regarding the five selfies he took with himself and the kitten. I absorb his elation before I open Ryder's. The ones I never checked a few days ago because I wanted to stay focused.

> **Ryder - Thursday @ 3:20pm:**
> I was going to be gone for six days, so I'll give you six, Elle. But that's it, not a fucking day longer.

> **Ryder - Thursday @ 6:30pm:**
> I take it back; I can't give you six days. Call me

> **Ryder - Thursday @ 6:45pm:**
> I'm waiting, and you know I'm not patient.

Ryder - Thursday @ 7:02pm:
I swear to god woman, if you don't answer your
phone I will make sure my handprint stays on
your ass for a fucking week.
Call me!

Ryder - Friday @ 3:02am:
I can't sleep, you're not here.
I miss you, and I love you.
Come home please.

Ryder - Friday @ 11:02am:
Time's up, beautiful.

Fuck.

I respond with a quick, *'I love you, handsome'* because
Tiny is at the bottom of the stairs waiting to go. You don't
make an old man like Tiny wait because as I said before, he
hasn't got much time left.

"Sorry old man hope you weren't waiting long," I say as I
give him a kiss on his old weathered cheek.

He shrugs. "If I was and I went, rather it be waitin' on a
pretty woman than doin' nothin' with those grumpy bastards."

I give him a big smile because he meant every bit of what
he said, and it makes me love him that much more. "C'mon
old man, I got a plane to catch."

Leading me out the door, he motions ahead to the black
Ford truck. I'm not surprised to see someone else driving us
because Tiny looks like he might fall asleep against the wheel
or possible fall asleep and never wake up.

Remy hops out, a hard-around-the-edges and beautiful man
of few words. He barely said two words to me last night but

that's who he is. He sits, stares, and remains broody until something is important enough to be verbal.

Surprising me, he takes my small suitcase and puts it in the backseat of the truck and opens the passenger door for Tiny. "I'm old, I ain't fuckin' dead yet," Tiny growls, batting Remy out of the way so he can get in the truck himself.

"Coulda' fooled me ol' man," Remy gripes.

Enjoying my own little laugh knowing I am not the only one who teases him about his age, I follow Norma into the back. Remy closes the door behind me.

"Cocksuckers don't know respect if it bit 'em in the ass," Tiny grumbles as he reclines his seat.

***

"What the hell kinda shit is that?"

"It's music, old man," Remy says.

"Can't hear no music, just people screamin'. That ain't music."

I don't put my two cents in because Godsmack is a favorite of mine. I also enjoy their bickering. I've never spoken much to Remy, mainly because he too hates useless chatter. But I'm beginning to think he's just selective with who he chatters with.

Remy pulls the truck into the small airport. "Where to, darlin'?"

I shake off the fog I was in. "Left after the gate," I tell him.

Driving where I tell him to go, he says, "you're a friend of Jimmy's."

It's not a question, but I answer him regardless, making eye contact in the rear-view mirror. "He's not my friend, he's my family."

Understanding, he nods. "He's good people."

Yes, he is. But that wasn't a question either and we've reached the end of this little journey. I open my door and hop out with Norma. Tiny fumbles around for a few minutes before him and Remy come around to the front of the truck. Remy hands off my suitcase to the flight attendant on the tarmac.

"Damn girl, you sure know how to travel don't ya?"

I roll my eyes at him. "I had to make sure Norm was comfortable."

He reaches down, fluffing my girl's fur. "Oh, she's comfy alright, and packs a pillow wherever she goes."

I ignore his comment about my husky girl and wrap my arms around him. "This is so long old man, take care of yourself."

His withering arms surround me, and he kisses me on the head. "So long girl, keep livin'."

I let go and give a small smile to Remy. "Thanks for the ride." He gives a chin lift. "Pleasure's mine, darlin'."

After a small salute, I board the plane, not entirely sure about what will happen next but knowing I have one last thing to do before my head will be cleared.

***

I'm thankful I dozed off on the plane. Even though I'm stubborn to admit it, I don't sleep well when Ryder isn't with me. I also don't sleep well when I have life changing shit on my mind. I stretch out in my seat, loving the luxury of flying privately. It's comfortable and spacious enough to catch up on some much-needed shuteye.

I stand up and stretch, waiting for the door to open so I can meet up with Brock. I texted him when I left to remind him of my arrival time. I know he wouldn't forget. There were no new texts from Ryder after his '*times up*' text he sent on Friday. Now it's Sunday but I have no idea what that meant.

I exit the plane with Norma, she scurries her fluffy body to the first patch of grass and does her business while I turn my phone back on. There's no sign of Brock, or my Chevelle so I bring up my text app seeing his name.

> **Brock - Sunday @ 10:50am:**
> *Did all I could do but he's a pushy fucker.*
> *Stay happy, talk soon.*
> *B*

Norma takes off, well, as fast as one her size can take off and I whistle. She slows but doesn't stop and I see the Chevelle come into view.

I look beyond it and notice the red white and blue flags hanging off the building, not like the building I took off from in Indianapolis. These flags aren't just the American ones either. Every flag bares the letters, 'NC'.

North Carolina.

I spin around and watch as the pilot pushes my bag toward me, not the flight attendant I didn't need. Noticeably uncomfortable he says, "forgive me, he's rather persuasive."

THE UGLY ROSES

I don't get a chance to reply when a deep voice washes over me. "Miss me, beautiful?"

I close my eyes and shiver like the horny hooker I am for this man before I turn around asking, "How?"

Of course, he smirks, but I can tell he's still pissed. "Like he said, I'm persuasive, and I told you time was up."

I huff, not necessarily annoyed because I'm actually pretty fucking impressed. Still I say, "you gave me six days, Ryder."

He shrugs. "I couldn't wait any longer."

I grab ahold of the handle on my luggage and start walking toward my car. I don't make it very far when he takes it from me and grabs hold of my arm, swinging me around. "No kiss, hello?"

He doesn't wait, he takes it. Like everything else in life, he grabs it by the horns and rides that bitch into the sunset. No holds barred, he takes whatever he wants and doesn't stop until I give it back.

When he's done, he grabs my hand and marches us to the car, tossing my suitcase in the trunk and of course opening my door for me because even though he's pissed, he's not quite an asshole and still has manners.

"Thank you," I mumble getting into the passenger seat. I could argue that it's my car and I want to drive but I don't really feel like driving because I'm kind of tired and still a little grumpy. When he gets in the driver's side, my stubbornness kicks in, or maybe it never really left; it was just dulled for a moment because he can kiss incredibly fucking well. Sometimes it leaves me stupid for a moment.

He knows it too.

Stubborn bitch on, I ask, "what if I wanted to say goodbye to Brock and Sam? And how did you get my car here? Do I want to even ask how you knew where I was?"

Starting the car, he puts it in drive. I know he wouldn't put it past me to get out and take a cab so it isn't until we pull on the highway when he responds. "You can invite them to our wedding and say goodbye then. I flew to Indie and picked up your car and drove it back, and I knew where you were because Brock called Denny and Denny called me, but I already knew you were there when Denny called. I tracked your phone and you texted Matty from Indianapolis."

I shake my head in disbelief. "Well don't leave anything out," I say, totally laced with sarcasm.

He nods, remembering something. "And Brock told me who you flew with so when I was in Indie, I redirected your flight. I told the pilot I wanted to surprise my future wife by taking some of the load off, not making her drive all the way home."

I watch his profile as he drives and take in everything he said. "Did you really want to take the load off or did you just want to avoid an awkward eleven-hour drive in the same car as me."

Taking his eyes off the road, he removes his sunglasses when we come to a stoplight to look at me. "I don't say shit that I don't mean, you know that Elle. You also know that I love you and regardless of how fucking stubborn you are I know I don't need to repeat that to remind you."

He pauses, allowing that to sink in before he continues. "That shit aside, I'm pissed you ran away from me, not toward me when something is clearly fucking with your head. I had a chat with Brock, he told me why you were there, and I get it beautiful, I do. You needed to set that shit straight and let your friends know who you really are so you can move on, but I'm asking you now, do not fucking run from me again. I don't like it and call me a goddamn pussy if you want but when you act like you don't need me, well that shit *burns*."

Taking his eyes off me he puts them back on the road, putting his sunglasses back on. He allows me to absorb everything he just said. I know I fucked up. Kind of. Okay, not a lot but I'm used to being on my own and he wasn't supposed to be home. I reverse the situation and I know I would be pissed if he didn't tell me where he was going, but half the time I don't know where he is or what he's doing either. I'm accepting of that because it's his job and I love him.

I don't currently have a job, but I do feel like what I did was more important than any job because it was incredibly important to me that I get that shit off my chest and open up my once closed off self to the people who helped me get where I am today.

Chapter Thirty

"I apologize for upsetting you Ryder, but I don't apologize for leaving. I didn't just need to do that, I had to."

There, that should placate him.

Or not, as I get no response. He stews in the driver's seat. My phone pings in my pocket and I glance over Brock's last message, now understanding what he meant. I send a quick 'no worries' before I move onto the next one. I can't help but smile when I see a text from Matty, but when I open it my eyes glaze over.

Not wasting another second, I call him, he answers on the second ring. "Gina?"

He's clearly upset. "Matty, what's wrong buddy? Your text wasn't a happy one today."

He sighs, "Sorry, Gina."

I correct myself. "Matty, you have nothing to apologize for. I just worry about you and I want to make sure you're okay, alright?"

"Okay, Gina." he replies, sounding defeated.

"What's wrong buddy, you can tell me."

He's silent for a moment and I swear I hear a sniffle. "We lost Bambi today, it was really sad."

"Who's Bambi, Matty?" I ask in a soft voice.
"A puppy, she had spots and Nancy let me name her Bambi. I brought her a ball this morning but when I got here, she was already gone."

I hate how defeated and upset he sounds. I want to hug him, but I know it won't cure the loss he just experienced. "Matty, has Nancy talked to you about how not all of the animals you try to help will make it? Sometimes they go to heaven earlier than we want them too." I hold back the sob as I get those words out, completely emotional as it's not lost on me that I am giving him advice that I too have learned the hard way.

"She did Gina, I'm just sad," he says.

I close my eyes, not bothering to wipe the tear that escapes. "It's okay to be sad, buddy. It's also okay to find ways to make up for it, sort of like moving on even though you don't forget because it just makes you work harder the next time. Does that make sense?"

"It makes sense. Like how I'm helping the kitten and she's doing really well. She won't take the bottle as good from Nancy. She says the kitten must really like me," he says with a little more spark in his voice.

Swallowing my emotion, I say, "that's exactly what I'm talking about Matty, I'm sure you're doing a great job."

I can hear his smile through the phone, not big, but a smile none the less. "Thanks, Gina. I'm going to go feed the other cats now while the kitten's sleeping. I'll call you soon."

"Do you need me to come and see you, Matty? If you need a friend, you know I will."

"No, that's okay. But you're coming to the barbecue, right?"

I truly smile into the phone. "I'll be there, I promise."

I hang up the phone and when Ryder asks what's wrong, I give him the short of it. Ryder lays a heavy hand on my thigh and leaves it there in silent support. Too choked up for more words I stare out the window until we get home.

***

I'd like to say I stopped crying, but I haven't. Silent tears run behind my sunglasses and down my cheeks. I grab the long sleeve of my black top and wipe my eyes, ignoring the fact I want to cry harder when I see the ring Ryder gave me.

I knew this was going to happen. I have changed. But apparently in many ways, I haven't. I don't notice it's time to get out yet until Ryder opens my door and crouches down beside me. Unbuckling my seatbelt, he swings my legs his way and inserts himself between them.

Removing the sunglasses from my face and already taking his off our eyes meet. "I know you love him, beautiful, and I know you missed him, but he's going to be okay."

His declaration makes my breath hitch and I put his face in my hands, rubbing my thumbs along the stubble, ignoring the snot that won't stop running from my nose.

"I know he will, but that's not it," I choke out, gasping for breath, watching the emotion in his eyes.
His eyes turn hard, determined. "What is it? You know I'll fix it. Just tell me, Elle. I don't know what to fix until you tell me."

God love this man in front of me and his sincerity. Truly he's the most remarkable man on the earth and he's all mine. I've been a bitch, but it was for my own selfish reasons because my head is like a goddamn rubix cube sometimes.

I needed to get away. I needed to think. I needed to clear my conscience and start this new life fresh. I needed to drop some of the baggage I didn't need and bring back what I would let Ryder help carry.

So, I decide to let out the only secret I've held from him. The last of me that he has yet to learn and hope to fuck he can guide me through this seeing as I have yet to overcome the anxiety.

"I'm pregnant, Ryder," comes out of my mouth on a whisper.

I watch as hope, shock and love take over his face before he lets out the breath he must have been holding. Shaking his head, disbelief and unshed tears spring from his eyes.

"But you can't? You couldn't? Fuck, I don't understand, Elle?"

Digging my fingers deep into his neck, I hold his head still, willing myself to get it out fast because he looks as if he's going to lose his shit if he doesn't get the answers fast enough.

"I was sick."

"What?" His head snaps up, furious eyes meet mine.
I shake my head. "No handsome, not like that. I just got sick the other day and I thought it was nerves." I swallow the lump before continuing. "My period's irregular but that's nothing new, and I was worried how Matty would settle in at Willow Beach, so I chalked it up to nerves."

He's focused, absorbing every word so I continue. "When I brought you and the guys lunch at work a few days ago I went into the clinic afterward. I thought I knew but I wasn't totally sure, so they did a scan and some blood tests."

I swallow again, allowing him a moment to take it in before I continue. "The blood tests showed that I was pregnant, and the scan showed my tubes had grown back together." I shake my head, still confused at the odds. "Ryder, apparently this only happens to like, *twelve* women out of a thousand, but a new passage formed and I'm pregnant." I rush out, not able to let him hang on any longer and scared to shit at what's going to happen.

I didn't want another child.

I can't have another child.

I'm scared.

I'm happy.

"I'm gonna be a father?" Ryder whispers, as if this conversation is too important to have in a high tone. Our voices have been hushed.

"You're going to be a father," I whisper back.

If I could bottle the smile spreading across his face, I would. It's the most beautiful smile I've ever seen, and it only adds to the tears running down my face.
"When?" he asks, pressing his lips to mine.

I press my lips to his, enjoying the taste of him and the saltiness of my tears as I respond, "According to the doctor, next August. And if he's right and the scan was accurate, we got pregnant at the beginning of last month."

I watch the wheels turn in his head. "I was only with you for a few days before I was gone for the week for work."

I nod my head, knowing what he means.

"You're telling me that I either got you pregnant when I asked you to be my wife, or the morning after. We didn't have sex for a week after that because you weren't feeling well and then I was gone for work."

I nod my head because he's right; I was spotting and wasn't feeling well. "That's what I'm telling you because that's what he told me."

"We're having a baby?" he asks.

I choke on my breath a little but reply, "we're having a baby."

After that I can't hold it in. The sobs, the emotion, the hope. It all runs out my eyes and surprisingly his too. Ryder lifts me out of the car, wrapping my legs around his body, pushing his hands into my hair, holding my face to his. "We're having a baby."

I sob against his mouth, not caring and neither does he I have snot running out of my nose. He just kisses me for all that he's worth and all that he has, and I take it. I take it all until he presses his forehead to mine and squeezes my body tight to his.

"Are you okay?" he asks.

I speak against his lips. "I wasn't at first, that's why I had to go, clean up my past and figure out how to start fresh."

"I'm sorry I was an asshole, beautiful."

I shake my head at him. "You love me, you weren't an asshole and I understand. Anyway, when I found out, didn't think I would be okay because it scared the shit out of me, but I am. I'm okay. I'm going to be a mom again and I'm okay."

Smiling against my mouth he says, "and I'm going to be a dad. I didn't think I could love this life anymore beautiful, and I'll always love you, but I have to say thank you. Thank fuck for you beautiful. I love you."

215

I smile against his handsome face. "And I still love the fuck out of you, Ryder Callaghan. Now take me home."

We're parked in our driveway, but that's not home. He knows home is us together, so I don't object when he walks me onto the back deck and lays me down on the outdoor couch, ridding my lower half of clothing so he can bury himself inside of me.

Wherever Ryder is, is home.

Our home.

Chapter Thirty-one

I walk up the few small steps, crossing the light blue painted porch. I don't knock yet because I'm too busy taking in the small things. The little porch swing just big enough for two people. The hostas we planted in the garden along with two begonias hanging baskets from the porch roof. It looks like any other duplex owned by someone who looks after it.

It's beyond normal.

It's perfect.

I take two more steps to the white front door and knock. It's a security door with a small window. The wooden porch door was propped open with a ceramic dog that reads, *Welcome.*

I wait, more nervous than I have been in I don't know how long. Why? I don't know, he'll be happy to see me. I debated barging in, but I wanted to give him his space, his own space, for the first time in his life.

I want him to have a choice before he lets someone in.

The security door opens, and I'm greeted with the biggest of smiles from the sweetest of men. I can't help but smile back because it's contagious. How could someone not smile back at that sweet face and bright eyes?

Impossible.

"Gina!"

I don't bother correcting him, I know I never will. I simply walk into the arms of the man who's but a child and half a foot taller than I am. It's not a manly embrace, it's a child's, one where he waits to be welcomed despite the fact I showed up at his home and he should be welcoming me.

He doesn't understand, and that's okay. More than okay as I seize the moment to squeeze him tighter than I have anyone in a while. I press a kiss above his ear and hold him as close as I can for as long as he'll let me.

"Happy Birthday, Matty."

"Thanks! I missed you, Gina! I called you because I finally got my present!"

Matty has going on and on about his *present*. His actual birthday is tomorrow but he wanted to celebrate today because they have a dog at Second Chance that is having surgery tomorrow and he doesn't want him to be alone.

That's my sweet Matty for you.

He never told me what his present was, just that it was a surprise and it was coming soon. It's not that I don't pay attention to him, I do. I pay more attention to Matty than I have many people in years.

However, sometimes I can't help when I forget. I don't mean to, never. I just have so much on my mind that it only holds the imperative stuff. I still have not completely gotten over my attack and that fucks with my head sometimes but it's rare. Mix that in with a pregnancy and I'm a regular hormonal head case. Complete with going to the store to buy milk and coming with everything but.

I allow Matty to pull me by the hand into his living quarters. I pass through the orange colored hallway and enter the light green living room which is off of a bright yellow kitchen. It's not at all my color but I asked Matty what he wanted, and where he wanted it. This house is what we ended up with. I didn't hire out the work, because I wanted to do something *with* him, not just *for* him. So, we painted some very unique colors that don't match at all but he loves it so we're happy.

"Look, Gina, look!"

I don't look at what Matty is pointing at, or who.

I can't.

Matty has a small living space and the patio out back is open, leading to a common area. It's there that I look. I can't take my eyes off them. The back-screen door is propped open giving me a clear view of the Callaghan Security men. Cabe, Maverick, Finn and Hunter, Ivan and Denny sit on the edge of a concrete planter. Finn and Hunter who I haven't had much time to spend with sit at the small table.

My eyes finally land on Ryder, standing next to a barbecue that clearly has something cooking on it for lunch.

"Did you see, Gina? Look at him!"

He's still pointing near the doorway to the living area, but my eyes are too watery to take it in. Ryder's lips tip up as Maverick lets out a whistle. Only then do I allow my eyes to follow the movement of white moving to the ground level patio.

"Come on Ry, come back here!" Matty says as he runs out of the house, chasing after the little white fluff of fur as Norma comes out from the distant water's edge. I cover my mouth when I reach the patio, overcome with emotion, hormones and happiness. Ryder's strong arms surround me, his large hands resting on my baby bump. "Calm, beautiful. He's well."

His words do anything but as I sob into his shirt sleeve, looking at all these strong men, enjoying a soda no less on my friends back patio. I hope they understand how much it means to Matty, because I can barely voice how much this mean to me.

219

I watch Matty run back up to the patio, his new little dog and Norma in tow. "Did you see that, Gina? Rydelle finally chased a stick and brought it back! Did you see that?"

I shake my head through my tears. "He's smart like his owner, Matty. Just like you, he's very smart." I try to keep the deep emotion out of my voice as well as the tears but it's impossible.

Matty shrugs as he nears. "He's *Rydelle*! He'll catch anything!"

Rydelle?

Bending down he scratches behind the Pyrenees's ears before looking at his new friends. "Did you see that, Denny? Cabe? Did you see?"

My man's men get up from where they lean and scrub a hand through *Rydelle's* fur and pat Matty on the back. "We saw it bud, good job. You're a natural trainer."

I watch as Matty's eyes light up, never having acceptance or praise like he's gotten from these men. I watch it settle into his eyes then his body like a warm blanket on a cold winter day.
"Thanks, friends," he says in a small quiet voice. Because that's what we are, friends, and Matty feels the need to verbalize it because he's never had any true ones.

I never introduced all these men to Matty, but here they are. With him, supporting him, being his friend. It means so fucking much to me and I can't help but reach out, putting my arms around Matty, letting him know no matter how many friends he has I will still be his first. I will always be his first and I will never leave him alone or let him go.

Naturally, he laughs when I hug him. He's used to my hormonal tendencies now. I want to laugh too but I can't. "It's okay Gina, Norma's been good, but I need my own dog now."

I let him believe that my tears fall because Norm will be coming home with me today. Matty asked to have her for a sleepover at his new home and I couldn't say no.

He smiles at me letting me in on the secret of how he got his dog. "That's why Ryder and all my new friends took me to the dog place for my birthday," he says. "I wanted to name him after a strong superhero, and Ryder told me the toughest superhero he knows is *Elle*, but that's Ryder's nickname for you so I told him my dog's name was gonna be *Rydelle*. Because he's the most baddest superhero guy I know. Like GI Joe, and he calls you Elle and you're the toughest superhero girl I know who helps people. Is it okay, Gina?" he rambles, "that I use your nickname for my dog? That I call my dog *Rydelle?"* He never stops to take a breath, and I have a hard time answering.

Rydelle.

Toughest people he knows.

Named after superheroes.

Matty gets distracted and before I know it, I'm in the middle of a group love. Ryder holding me to his chest, Denny's hand on my shoulder and the rest of them hold a hand to my back

"H-ehe-he's too good. He only deserves good and you guys gave that to him. You gave him what he's never had. Do you realize what this means to him? I feel like he'll finally be okay."

I pull out of Ryders embrace and take in the stoic faces of the men around me. Their misty eyes don't linger on mine too

221

long before they revert to their usual badass and drift toward Matty.

It's impossible not to.

His affection is contagious.

We watch him run along the patio edge with his new dog that's a spitting image of Norma. He giggles like a child when the puppy jumps up to lick him. Norm knocks the puppy out of the way so she can seek her attention.

Ryder's lips find mine and his hand cradles my pregnant stomach as he responds, "it's not just okay beautiful, it's perfect."

***

After hot dogs, as per Matty's request, I balled my face off like a whiny bitch for the rest of the afternoon while I watched him interact with the men from Callaghan Security and some of the other residents at Willow Beach.

I wish there was a pill I could take that would stop the water running from my eyes. If I'm not crying, I'm bitching at someone. It's usually Ryder, but like a trooper he takes it. When he doesn't take it, well...let's just sum it up and say my ass gets his handprint.

I don't complain.

Ever.

That man's hands are magic and so long as they are on me you won't hear me bitching.

THE UGLY ROSES

We all pile into our vehicles, the men in their badass trucks and SUV's, and Ryder, Matty and I into my kickass car. I told Matty I would take him wherever he wanted to go for his birthday dinner, and he asked, very politely, to go to the place he rides past on his bike that has the fish tank in the window.

After a quick cleanup of my face, I re-applied my mascara and fixed my loose plum colored tunic top over my little baby bump and called myself good to go.

Ryder puts his arm around me, ever the protective one and we walk behind the crew toward the restaurant. I ignore the hussies who can't walk in heels, drooling over my fine group of men as we enter Hook and Sinker. I hear Denny tell the hostess about our reservation. She says it will just be a few minutes.

Matty walks over to the fish he was dying to see, naming each one because he researched what they were when he first became intrigued with them. I listen as he tells Cabe how long some of them live and what their purpose in the sea is, until the hussy's conversation from the parking lot grabs my attention.

"What is he, like twelve?" asks tan in a can.

"I bet you he's gay," replies Elvira. And that's a compliment coming from me because everyone knows Elvira had kickass, black hair, not dried out and teased poorly like hers.

Yes, you can tease poorly.

I breathe in through my nose, knowing I'm back and I feel fucking good about it because for once I'm not crying.

I breathe out at the same time Ryder says, "fuck me," and Denny says, "shit." Hunter says, "this is going to be fucking good," with a shit eatin' grin on his face directed my way.

Standing a little taller in my fuck-me black boots, I turn to face the useless hussies with a smile, albeit a condescending one.

"You know it's unfortunate when people like yourselves are so uncomfortable in their own skin they need to pick on others. He can't stand up for himself, but I'm happy to admit that I have enough balls and comfort in my own skin to do it for him.

"You see, he can't go home and change who he is like you can go home and change the shirt that's two sizes two small, or that birds nest you call a hair do. Because, let's face it sweetheart, they are fixable."

I allow that to sink in. "My Matty can't change a lot, but that's perfectly fine because we all love him just the way he is. So, while you're standing there, judging and thinking you're better than him, I'm going to give you some advice," I wave my hand out, "words of wisdom actually, to help you navigate adulthood since you clearly haven't progressed from being a child."

Two stunned faces stare at me as I carry on, "So here are three things: first off," I say facing tan in a can, "if you can't own 'em, don't wear 'em. I watched you weave your way in here. Clearly stilettos aren't for you since you had the whole tipsy teenager thing going on. My advice is to wear flats and work your way up."

Smiling, I turn to Elvira wannabe. "Second, check your judgments and attitude at the door. Nobody in this place wants to hear it and it won't get you good service." I eye the hostess and what I assume is the manager who have joined the impromptu hussy roast. "Not because this establishment isn't capable of providing good service, it's because us decent people came to eat or work here, not to listen to your childish yap while we pay top dollar for some of the freshest seafood off the coast."

Pausing, I allow all *that* to sink the fuck in because they still look like two-dollar hookers in the headlights before I continue. "The third, is if you can't do the first two, then take your tipsy teenager, judgmental, ignorant hussy asses somewhere else where you *might* fit in. But word of advice, sweetheart." I lean in closer. "Fill your tank before you go, 'cause you'll be driving a long fucking time before you find it."

I ignore the tears gathering in tan in a can's eyes as I head to the hostess station. "I believe our table should be ready now?"

She's flustered, fighting her smile and shaking off what she just witnessed when she stutters, "y-yes, right this way."

"I fucking love pregnant women," says Hunter.

"You want to live to look at them, you'll shut your fucking trap," says Ryder.

I ignore them both and grab Matty who thankfully was oblivious to what went on because he was too engrossed in checking out the fish.

Chapter Thirty-two

"Thanks, friend!" Matty exclaims as he studies the dog brush and toys that Hunter and Finn gave him for his birthday. I'm happy they didn't do something Hunter and Finn'ish—like rent him a hooker for his 30th.

Small miracles.

Denny got him a cordless drill. I'm happy he paid attention when we were helping Matty decorate his home. He was uncomfortable when we kept driving to the store for small things that he needed, even something as simple as a hammer to hang a few animal prints on the wall. Matty likes to be prepared, and now he has one more thing to make him feel that he is.

"Here buddy," I say, handing over mine and Ryder's present. I know Ryder bought him his dog, but this is still from us.

Matty eagerly tears the bright blue paper off the box before he lifts the lid. In true Matty fashion, he handles each gift with care as he sets them on the table. I put my arm across his back, watching his sweet face as he takes in all that's inside.

There are ten photo frames in total, along with the pattern to hang them.

"How, Gina?" Matty quietly asks.

I control my pregnancy sobs and explain. "Every year you were in school Matty, they took your picture. Do you remember that?"

He nods his head, so I continue. "I noticed you didn't have any of those pictures, so Ryder and Cabe helped me get them and I put them in the frames for you."

I watch as he slowly takes out a few photos he did have, of him and Miss Marion. I framed the best ones I could find and they're beautiful. Folding over the last layer of tissue paper he sees the last photo of himself, Ryder, Norma and me. It was taken by a fisherman when Ryder and I took him to the docks a few weeks ago. The sun is setting in the background and we all have happy smiles on our faces, my arm around Matty, his other hand on Norma and Ryder's hand resting on my baby bump.

His voice is deeper, more mature, and full of emotion when his tear-filled eyes meet mine. "Thank you. Just...thank you."

Don't just survive.

Live.

"You're very welcome Matty."

***

"Ryder don't you dare fucking tease me," I warn. He got home last night from a job up in Virginia. He was only gone for two nights but being pregnant makes me hornier than a teenager. The three orgasms he gave me last night were wonderful, and needed, but this morning is a whole new day.

I can't get it enough.

I can't have him enough.

"Ryder!" I reach out and tangle my fingers in his hair, pulling it tight to the roots just the way he likes it. He's been going down on me for the better part of the morning, but every time I get close to the edge, he pulls me back.

That devious smirk is on his face. "It's payback."

I shake my head. "What in the hell are you talking about? This isn't payback, it's torture! There's a big difference, Callaghan!"

He plants a kiss on my thigh. "You going to listen to me now?"

"I have no idea what you're talking about," I huff, laying back on the bed. Frustrated he's not looking after me I move my hand over my baby bump prepared to finish it myself.

"Ah ah, not happening," Ryder growls as he grabs my wrists and pins them beside my head. Leaning over me he keeps his lips, wet with my arousal, inches from my face.

"I asked you to do one thing, Elle. One thing."

I ignore him, lifting my hips hoping to gain some friction but he pulls further away. "Dammit, Ryder!"

He shakes his head. "Not this time, Elle. I fucking asked you, then I told you because you didn't listen when I asked. You're still not listening."

A growl comes from somewhere in my throat. I was a bit of a miserable bitch before who lacked patience. Being pregnant amplified both of those traits and now I have no patience at all.

"For fuck's sake Ryder, just tell me what it is. I'll say sorry and then you can fuck me."

Clearly still pissed at me he remains where he is and says, "I fucking told you Elle, if you need help with the security system call any one of the guys. If you need help around the house call anyone but Hunter. Why couldn't you do that?"

I'm confused and ignore everything he said except the last part. "Why can't I call Hunter?"

He purses his lips and scowls. "Because good looking pregnant women get his dick hard."

I can't help it, I laugh. "I thought every kind of woman got Hunter's dick hard?"

He tightens his hold on my wrists and leans closer to my face. "Don't talk about Hunter's dick in our bed."

I scoff. "You just did."

"Ya, I did and if you don't stop doing it, you're not getting mine."

I soften my eyes, sighing his name in a way I know gets him hard. "Ry, please." I even add an eyelash flutter but sadly, it doesn't work.

"Not fallin' for that shit, Elle. I told you if you needed help to call for it. You didn't and that pisses me off."

"What the hell did I need help for?"

He scowls. "What's with the tools on top of the washing machine?"

"The hot water line was leaking again so when I was at the hardware store, I bought a new clamp to put on it. No big deal, it's fixed."

He's not happy it's fixed because he's still scowling at me. "What about the truckload of plants that are sitting on the deck, and the multitude of planters?"

I sigh. "I told you a long time ago you needed some landscaping and curb appeal. So, when I was at the hardware store I picked up the red planters and they had a sale on annuals so I picked up some plants. What's the big deal?"

"Who loaded all that heavy shit into the truck, Elle?"

I frown. "The dude at the hardware store and the chick who worked the garden center."

Leaning down so our noses are touching he says, "and who unloaded it all when you got home?"

I bite my cheek. "I did."

Without any help from his hands because he's hard as a rock he surges forward, entering me in one quick thrust.

"Gah! Thank you!"

He pounds into me, once, twice. I'm so worked up I nearly blow.

But he pulls out.

"No!"

He smirks. "Tell me you'll call one of the guys for help next time."

I shake my head. "I'm fucking pregnant, Ryder. Not handicapped!"

He puts his hand down between us, circling my clit with his thumb. "Tell me you'll ask for help."

"I can't sit on my ass all day, Ryder." I sigh, loving his magical fingers until he takes those away from me too.

"You don't sit on your ass all day, and you work yourself too hard."

"Dammit Ryder, the only thing I can do is a light jog and Pilates. You know I can't sleep unless I physically exert myself."

"You sleep just fine when I'm home," he says.

"That's because you fuck me to sleep, Ryder," I tell him.

His face turns serious. "You telling me you don't sleep when I'm gone?"

I shake my head. "Not well. I manage I guess but it's always better when you're here."

His eyes soften and I'm happy to say that does the trick as he surges forward and presses his lips to mine.

"Ask for help, beautiful."

I sigh, not wanting to give in but knowing Ryder won't stop until he wins. Since I have no patience and want an orgasm more than my next breath, I agree. "On one condition—two actually."

He smirks, rolling his hips into mine. "What are they?"
My eyes roll back into my head. "Two orgasms before we leave today, and you have to get me those cream-filled pastry thingies that Cabe brought me last week."

Warm lips devour mine and I have no doubt he will make good on both of my requests.

Chapter Thirty-three

Ryder

She wanted pastries?

I got her fucking pastries.

I'll get her anything she wants, and she knows I'll do it with a smile on my face because I'm the luckiest son of a bitch on the planet.

I roll up the sleeves on my black dress shirt as I walk from the bathroom to the closet where Elle is. I gave her the two orgasms she requested this morning, I'm sure she knows I would have given them to her regardless of whether she agreed with me or not. I fucking love that woman, and putting a smile on her face, watching her come apart beneath me are two of my favorite things in the whole world.

Her makeup is already done, her wild mess of blonde and brown hair is loose and flowing down her back. I smile as I watch her from the doorway. She's huffing, something, she does that a lot lately when she's trying to get her pants on and complains that *nothing fucking fits!*

"Need some help, beautiful?"

Her evil eyes swing toward mine and she stills for a moment, hands on the pants that she's currently trying to pull over her luscious ass and failing miserably. "Don't, Callaghan. Don't you dare fucking say it."

Blowing the hair off her face, she continues to fight with her pants. This has been going on for months now. Elle is not a woman you can talk into wearing a dress out in public without wearing tights or whatever the fuck she calls them underneath.

At home is a different story and putting her fine ass into a dress without pants or panties is a favorite pastime of mine.

If she doesn't hurry up, we're going to be late. As much as I don't mind waiting on her I head into the lion's den, prepared to take whatever shit she gives me but not willing to watch her battle with her pants any longer. Since she's already seated on the stool, I kneel down and grab the tights from her hips and pull them off her legs.

"What the hell Ryder, I almost had it!" she whines. If she's not whining lately, she's bitching, if she's not bitching she's crying. The only time she stops is when I hold her or fuck her and I'm completely okay with that.

I set my determined eyes on her glassy ones. "No beautiful, you did *not* have it." I grab her by the arms and pull her up, letting the green summer dress she has on fall to just above her knees before I pick her up in a bridal carry and head out of our room. "It's Denny's birthday, Elle. I'm not missing it just because you're struggling to put pants on that you don't need."

She huffs, but I notice she's just too tired to argue. I hate that she doesn't sleep well when I'm gone, hopefully I can start sending the guys on the out of town jobs and focus more on being at home, especially once the baby arrives which could happen any day now.

I'll never forget the first ultrasound.

Fuck, I'll never forget any of them and I made sure I was there for every single one. There's something surreal about hearing your child's heart beat for the first time. Never had I felt so proud. Proud of the strong woman Elle has become and proud with myself. I spent a long time as a bachelor with no intention of changing—until Elle came along. She surprises me daily; no moment is a dull one and I thank my lucky fuckin' stars that this is the woman I get to have a family with.

"Ryder, I need my shoes," she finally says as I walk out the back door with her still in my arms. The small get together for Denny's birthday is at the little cottage beside mine that Elle used to rent.

Beautiful, we're going next door, you don't need shoes." As usual, she huffs at me.

There are some things she lets go, but for the most part she argues with me at every damn turn. The only thing she doesn't argue with me about lately is food, and that's only because whatever you place in front of her she'll eat. She still maintains a good workout schedule, but I'd be lying if I said I won't miss her pregnant body. A little more ass, a beautiful bump that carries my child, and tits I can't get enough of.

"If you keep staring at my tits instead of where we're going, you're going to trip on something," she says.

I chuckle and set her on her feet making the last few steps to Denny's back porch. "About fucking time, I'm starving!" Finn complains from where he waits at the table. Denny replaced Elle's small table for four with something bigger for entertaining.

Elle takes no offense to Finn's jab at her tardiness as she sits down at the table. "Me too!"

Taking the seat next to her, she automatically puts her feet in my lap as Cabe hands her a tray of different meats and cheeses. "Thanks, Cabe," she mumbles around a mouthful, balancing the tray on her belly, not bothering to pass it around to anyone else.

Finn opens his big mouth, ready to argue with her for not sharing. The smart shit wisely snaps it closed when I glare at him. The only time Elle isn't arguing, crying, or mouthing off in the presence of others is when she's eating, and as much as I put up with all that shit, sometimes the silence is a blessing.

"Oh my god, are you pregnant?" Asks the bimbo sitting beside Hunter. I'm not sure who she is, he seldom brings women into the fold unless he plans on fucking them more than once.

Everyone is quiet as they wait for Elle's response. She's become mother hen to my guys; saying it like it is and never putting up with the less than intelligent women they bring around.

She swallows the cheese she had in her mouth before she speaks. "Actually, I'm just heavy and don't know how to put the fork down since I quit smoking."

Bimbo has the nerve to look at her with sympathy before she comes around the table and sits on the other side of Elle. "Oh my god, you should try this new diet a friend of mine is on…"

I don't listen, but like the rest of my men I keep my eyes on Elle, anticipating what will come out of her foul mouth next. Setting the now empty food tray on the table, Elle stands up, towering over the idiot in the chair as she continues to ramble about how important a no carb diet is.

"You know, Sally…"

"Sarah," she corrects.
Elle smirks. "Right, Sarah. I am feeling a little crampy, maybe I should have shared the meat and cheese platter instead of hogging it to my heavy self."

Sarah nods. "That's the first step, knowing when enough is—AHHHHH!"

I watch the gush of water fall between my wife's legs, soaking the deck and the shoes of the idiot broad in front of her.

"Ooops," Elle says with a smile.

I'm too shocked to move until Sarah shouts. "Did you just piss on me?"

The smirk vanishes from Elle's face. "No, you dumb shit, I'm pregnant! Now get the hell out of here unless you want blood on those heels too!"

I grab her by the shoulders. "Shit! Jesus, we need to get to the hospital."

Elle shakes her head. "I'm fine handsome, wait until the contractions start."

I press my lips to hers. "I love you, fuck! I'm gonna be a dad."

She leans up on her toes to deepen the kiss before she lets out the most blood curdling scream, falling toward the ground. But as always, I catch her.

I'll always catch her.

Epilogue

How did I get here?

I know the answer without too much thought when warm hands settle over my baby bump, his thumbs moving slowly over the soft material of my ivory maxi dress.

It's taken a long time to get where I am, and even longer for me to believe it. That's the thing about the heart, you can tell yourself one thing but at the end of the day until your heart and your mind catch up and meet in the same place, everything seems surreal.

Was I held in a basement and tortured for three days?

Yes, I was.

I was also violated and beaten in a jail cell, not to be topped by the most horrific of past experiences when I was but a moment away from being taken against my will—in every form of the word.

I won't dare say that everything happens for a reason. There was no reason for any of that awful shit to happen to my family or myself. The fact I'm still sitting here today only proves that I prevailed, I made the most of what is left and I'm where I'm supposed to be.

Fortunate.

Loved.

These past few years I have lived with the mindset that if you don't fear death, then it won't hurt. I lived that way because I felt as though I had nothing left to live for. For some fucked up reason it didn't stop me from fighting to stay alive.

I've fought with everything I have and everything in me believing the sole reason I did it was for retribution for my family, and perhaps justice for myself.

Little did I know that fighting would get me *here.* Call it fate, call it kismet, call it whatever you want. But when I moved into that little cottage in North Carolina I was exactly where I needed to be. Of course, I didn't know it at the time, and it was a long journey to get there with many people guiding me along the way.

I still miss my family; their death doesn't go away and there are days when it doesn't hurt any less. But I appreciate what I had more now than I did a few years ago. That's the problem with anger, one of the many stages of grief. It eats you alive until you're but a shell fighting against yourself rather than giving in.

Finding out that Andrew was responsible for killing my family took away from the happy memories I held, replacing them with a constant burn that turned me into the ice-cold bitch I once was. Surrounded by hate, wine, and overflowing ashtrays of stress was my way to self-medicate, numbing myself to any feeling other than hate.

I'd say that I'm ashamed of who I turned into, but I'm not. I've never denied who I am and that part of me, that year of walking around with cement boots fighting against the current of water is what made me who I am today.

I'm not entirely proud of my actions and I'm not content with the way I've treated some people by blocking them out and closing every door that was left open for me. However, at the end of the day, I know I'll always be stubborn, and I'll always be me. While some might lean on the first willing shoulder to cry on, I'll be the first to turn away.

Asking for help has never been my forte, and I don't suspect that will change. It's gotten better over time, but there are some things that can't be removed; taking the stubborn out of my Irish roots is one of them.

"Wiwy!"

I lean back against Ryder's chest, stretching my legs out on the freshly cut grass. His deep chuckle vibrates against my back and I can't help but smile while correcting him.

"*Lilly*, handsome boy," I correct him, with emphasis on the 'L' that he has trouble pronouncing. He gives me the trademark Callaghan smirk before scooting around and continuing his task.

Ryder's arms tighten around me as we watch our sweet boy waddle between headstones, leaving a string of flowers in his wake. It's not organized, it's completely messy and absolutely beautiful.

Jackson Matthew Callaghan was born almost two years ago in the very place I found my solace. Another full circle moment giving me back an emotion that I never thought myself worthy of again.

Peace.

"Fuck they're coming beautiful, hang on!"

Ryder tries to move me from my spot on the deck, but I cry out from the pain between my legs. "Ahhh!"

'Get something to lay her down on!" Cabe barks. I notice Denny grabbing a single lounge cushion, laying it down on the deck.

"Everyone stays behind her fucking head!" Ryder growls, shifting me so I lean against Denny before he crawls back between my legs.

"Arrgghhhh!" I scream, tears threatening to pour over.

Ryder wipes the sweat from his brow before putting his hands on my knees. "Gotta look, Elle."

I nod my head, watching Cabe toss a handful of towels at him before grabbing my hand. I try to stop myself from panicking. I had a quick labor with Lilly and this being my second child could be even quicker. I ignore all thoughts that something could be wrong, that this is moving too fast. I breathe in through my nose, out through my mouth looking at Ryder and the view behind him.

It's the same view I stared at for months, the one that got me here, the one that unknowingly answered my questions and prayers. I was blinded by a cruel fate for so long but I'm still here!

I allow that to sink in, penetrating my bones and warming my soul. Fate would never be so cruel as to take something else from me and the beautiful man with the halo of horizon behind him.

"I see the head, beautiful."

There is shock and awe on his handsome face, staring at me, waiting for me to say something to ease his worry as Hunter barks on his phone in the background to who I assume is an emergency dispatcher.
I relax, letting my mother instinct take over.

I've done this before.

I can do it again.

Allowing a small smile to grace my lips I reach for his face, pulling him toward me. Pressing my lips to his and keeping my greens on his blacks. "I love you, handsome, we can do this." I whisper, "Now get back down there because I need to push."

THE UGLY ROSES

His strong hand squeezes the back of my neck, firmly sealing his mouth to mine before he resumes his position. Placing one hand on my thigh, and the other between my legs, he nods.

So, I push.

Watching the tears stream down his rugged face as he lifts a dark haired, howling baby boy from between my legs fills every last crack in my once ice-cold heart. The cord is still attached as he moves over me, resting the beautiful boy on my chest, cocooned between us. The mop of dark hair is just like his fathers along with the dark skin. I study his sharp nose, small chin, and hope the lightness in his eyes will at least give him my green ones.

"Jackson," he says in a hoarse voice.

My questioning eyes leave my child to focus on his watering black ones.

"I laid eyes on the rest of my life one sunny day in Jacksonville. She almost ran me over, but it didn't stop me from chasing her."

I choke out a small sob through my happy tears. "Jackson," I whisper.

We don't listen to the hoots and hollers from the guys, or the paramedics as they take over. In that moment it was just us, and a sweet little miracle that would one day call me momma.

"He's growing too fast," Ryder says, placing a kiss on this side of my head. "Come back here little man!" he shouts, keeping his mini-me in line before he decorates the entire cemetery like a flower girl. Petals of all colors decorating the green and grey landscape.

Ryder is an amazing father, but I expected no less so I can't say that I'm surprised. He's firm when he needs to be with a healthy amount of nurturing. However, the men from Callaghan Security would agree with me when I say that I wear the pants when it comes to the parenting.

Jackson has his Daddy wrapped around his little pudgy finger.

I sigh. "He is, handsome. But I think we'll be grateful he's so big when Callaghan number two gets here. At least Jackson's potty trained."

Ryder chuckles behind me. "He had a good teacher."

I smile shaking my head. The day I walked into the bathroom and saw Jackson with his mini-potty beside his daddy's big potty nearly killed me. Naturally, my little boy has no aim, but that didn't stop him from following in his father's footsteps—literally—to pee like a big boy.

"MumMum," Jackson says, pointing at me and back to the tombstone. I smile and reach my hand out, beckoning him closer so I can hold him. Falling into my arms, I hold him tight. "Yes baby, I'm Lilly's mom too."

Smiling up at me he places his chubby hands on my cheeks, squealing when Ryder pulls us both close, giving him a raspberry on his neck.

"Dadda, 'top!" he giggles, trying to say *stop*, but we both know he loves it.

Settling down between my legs with his sippy cup, I run my fingers through his black hair, lacing the fingers on my other hand with Ryder's. I relish these moments, my strong handsome man behind me and a sweet little boy in our arms. There isn't a day that goes by that I don't remind myself how fortunate I am to have come this far.

THE UGLY ROSES

I went from having little family to having a big one. While most may not call it conventional, it means the world to me. My blood family may not be with me anymore, but it doesn't mean I don't appreciate and love the one that I have. The men from Callaghan Security along with Matty have truly filled my heart. I'm grateful that Jackson has many uncles to look up to, so many strong men to learn from. I couldn't have asked for better role models in my son's life.

In a few more months we'll meet our newest addition to the Callaghan crew. Once again, we decided not to find out what we're having. Either will make me happy and proud, but I pity the poor lass if it's a girl, she would stand little chance at ever going on a date with her broody uncles around.

"Humgy, MumMum," Jackson mumbles around his cup.

"C'mon beautiful, looks like everything's set up."

Ryder helps me up and I glance across the street to the park. Jimmy, Laura, Brad and the kids have gathered around one of the picnic tables. This is our last night in Ontario, and our farewell picnic will be the last time we eat together for a while once the baby gets here.

I press my fingers to my lips, and then lay them on the stone.

Lilly Jayne O'Connor

I'll always miss my baby girl, that will never go away, and I don't want it to. I need to remember and talk about her often to keep those memories alive. She deserves that and so much more. It's therapeutic to me now, sharing silly stories about her with Ryder. —It's also heartwarming the way Jackson mixes his potatoes and veggies and naps on Norma's belly— just like Lilly used to.

Small miracles.

"Buh bye, Wiwy," Jackson says, blowing wet kisses to the lonely stones.

We don't visit often, not just because we live so far away, but because I don't feel the need to be here all the time like I did when my family was killed. It took a while, but I know that I carry them with me wherever I go. I don't need to see the stone to remind me what I lost, or where they are now.

I could never forget.

A warm breeze floats through the maze of marble and stone, lifting the flower petals Jackson dropped and twirling them in the air. His giggle echoes through the cemetery and only when he quiets do the petals resume their resting place.

Ryder's arms surround me, providing the support I love and the strength I don't need at the moment because I *know*.

I *know* that this farewell isn't to remind me of loss and death, or the nightmares of my past.

This farewell is a reminder for what I have, not what I'm missing.

Not what I've lost.

The warm breeze is a blanket to my soul, the following calm a reassurance to my heart that heaven is taking care of my loves, and they're okay.

I can move on.

Move forward with my beautiful new family and focus on now, not four years ago or yesterday.

Because *now* is Ryder's arm around me, his large hand resting on the side of my belly where mini Callaghan number two is kicking.

THE UGLY ROSES

Now is his strong hand, holding a tiny little chubby one as we exit the land of the lost but never forgotten.

Now is this moment, when his handsome face turns, and his lips touch mine.

"I love you, Elle Callaghan."

This right here, the moment, the memory, the pain no longer present and the nightmares long since vanished—is living.

"Everybody needs to live girl, life ain't just about survivin' 'cause ya ain't got a life until you live." Tiny said.

Don't just survive.

Live.

No truer words were spoken.

Author Notes

Thank you so much for reading the final
Book of The Ugly Roses Trilogy. If you enjoyed it,
please take the time to leave a review on Amazon or
Goodreads.

Is *The Ugly Roses* over? No!
The Callaghan Security crew are next.
First up: Denver 'Denny' Black

You can learn about his book, The Lesser Half, on
Goodreads.

Want to chat about all thing's books?
Connect with Harlow:

HARLOW STONE

www.facebook.com/harlow.stone.author

harlow.stone.books@gmail.com

Instagram.com/harlowstone

www.harlowstone.com

Acknowledgments

Maryse's blog, because you were the first person to ever make a post about my book and I'll always be grateful for that.

Sutter Home Wine, no words can express how much you helped me complete this journey.

Freya Barker, you are an incredibly talented woman and the first to put up with my ridiculous questions regarding being a new author. Your support and wisdom have been truly appreciated and not forgotten.

Rachel Green, as per usual your peepers are the first to notice what's missing and I thank you for that. You're also my biggest backdoor-book-bootlegger so keep up the great work!

Christine Stanley from The Hype PR, first to dive in and support me to make The Ugly Roses *known* because *'people need to read this series'!* You rock!

My editor Greg, Great job and thank you for all your help on this journey.

And my readers, thank you, thank you, thank you.

Keep it classy,
Harlow
xx

Made in the USA
Middletown, DE
25 February 2021